11329

823.09

YORK NOTES

General Editors: Professor A.N. Jeffares (*University of Stirling*) & Professor Suheil Bushrui (*American University of Beirut*)

Thomas Hardy

THE MAYOR OF CASTERBRIDGE

Notes by Hilda D. Spear

MA (LONDON) PH D (LEICESTER) FIBA
Lecturer in English and Senior Adviser of Studies, University of Dundee

  LONGMAN
YORK PRESS

YORK PRESS
Immeuble Esseily, Place Riad Solh, Beirut.

LONGMAN GROUP UK LIMITED
Longman House, Burnt Mill, Harlow,
Essex CM20 2JE, England
Associated companies, branches and representatives
throughout the world

First published 1980
Sixth impression 1989

ISBN 0-582-02282-7

Produced by Longman Group (FE) Ltd.
Printed in Hong Kong

Contents

Part 1

Introduction

For most of his life Hardy lived and worked in that part of England about which he wrote so movingly and so powerfully in his novels and poetry. He was born on 2 June 1840 in the small village of Higher Bockhampton, near the county town of Dorchester, the 'Casterbridge' of his novels. From his mother he inherited a love of books of all kinds and from his father a sensitivity to music and an interest in building and stonemasonry that led him at the age of sixteen into the profession of architecture. After an apprenticeship in Dorchester he went to London in 1862 and there worked as assistant to an architect, Arthur Blomfield, helping him to restore and design churches.

Whilst working in London he began to write poetry and, indeed, for a while sent his manuscripts to various magazines; they were, however, so consistently rejected that he continued to write poetry merely for his own pleasure, storing away what he thought was worthwhile, destroying what he thought was mediocre. It was not until 1898 that his first volume of poetry, *Wessex Poems*, was published. Meanwhile, a bout of ill-health had forced him to abandon London and return to Dorset where he went to work as assistant to John Hicks in whose office he had served his apprenticeship. Simultaneously he abandoned poetry for prose and during 1867 and 1868 he wrote his first novel, *The Poor Man and the Lady*. This was, apparently, a social satire, but for a variety of reasons it was never published and the manuscript was finally lost or destroyed. Hardy received enough encouragement, however, from the readers of his manuscript, including the novelist George Meredith (1828–1909), to embark upon a second novel, this time a love story full of melodramatic and improbable incidents. This he called *Desperate Remedies*, and it was published anonymously at his own expense in the early months of 1871. The following year his second novel, *Under the Greenwood Tree*, was published. This is a gentle pastoral comedy, a complete contrast to the previous novel. It was well received by the reviewers and, though it is perhaps sometimes underestimated today, it is a novel of rare simplicity and charm; the group of simple country characters, generally called 'Hardy's rustic chorus', is displayed with humour and affection and there is a foreshadowing of a number of the more serious themes which are developed in his later novels.

The early 1870s were a time when not only his literary fortunes, but also his personal life were undergoing changes for, whilst employed on the renovations of the church of St Juliot, near Boscastle in Cornwall, Hardy met the rector's sister-in-law, Emma Lavinia Gifford, and fell in love with her. They were married in September 1874 and went to live in Surbiton, then a pleasant country suburb of London.

Hardy had by now decided to abandon his career as an architect and give himself up entirely to writing. His third novel, *A Pair of Blue Eyes*, had been published in 1873. Throughout the greater part of 1874 *Far From the Madding Crowd* had been serialised in *The Cornhill* and in the November after his marriage it was published complete in two volumes. This book was not only an instant success, but it also became the basis of Hardy's literary reputation. A more substantial novel than *Under the Greenwood Tree*, its balanced treatment of the themes which came to dominate his other major novels preserves it from many of the criticisms his later works attract.

During the next ten years the Hardys lived an unsettled life, moving first back to Dorset and a house in Sturminster Newton on the Stour, back again to London, then to Wimborne and finally to Dorchester where Hardy decided to build himself a house, Max Gate, which was to be his home for the rest of his life, though he continued to make annual visits to London. By the time he moved into Max Gate he had published nine novels and was preparing *The Mayor of Casterbridge* for serial publication. On his visits to London he was made much of and, one of the famous himself, he mixed with the famous, meeting familiarly such well-known figures as Matthew Arnold, Robert Browning, Henry James, George Meredith, Walter Pater, Lord Tennyson and Oscar Wilde; back home in Max Gate he entertained Robert Louis Stevenson. Emma, who had encouraged him in his early literary leanings, found that being the wife of a famous man was not all pleasure. Perhaps slightly odd to begin with, she grew more and more eccentric. The marriage remained childless. Hardy frequently visited London and went into company without her; his diaries and letters contain accounts of the beautiful women he had dined with and who constantly flocked to see him. Whether or not he would have liked to break his own marriage bond, he became increasingly critical of the legal obligations and the moral implications of marriage in his writings.

Hardy's last two novels, *Tess of the D'Urbervilles* (1891) and *Jude the Obscure* (1896), met with considerable hostility from the reviewers and though he refused to answer their criticisms he was puzzled at the widespread misunderstandings of both his meanings and his intentions. However, he had in the past few years been turning his attention increasingly to writing poems and now he decided to give up novel-writing and return to poetry, collecting together all the pieces he had preserved from about 1865 onwards for the edition of *Wessex Poems*. For some years, certainly since 1891, when he had first jotted down a few notes about it in his diary, Hardy had been considering writing a great epic drama on Europe during the period of the Napoleonic wars. This became *The Dynasts*, the first part of which was published in 1903 and the third and final part in 1908.

It was in 1904 that he first met Florence Dugdale who, ten years later, was to become his second wife. Almost forty years younger than he, she was a great help and comfort to him, acting as his secretary and managing and organising his household. His attachment for her grew and she became more and more indispensable to him, particularly as his wife appeared to be both spiritually and emotionally estranged from him. With little warning, though she had been somewhat unwell during the preceding months, Emma died in November 1912 and Florence Dugdale went to Max Gate to help Hardy over the time of his bereavement. The unexpected loss of Emma opened for him the floodgates of regret, of grief and of creative energy. The moving memory of past love, the kindliness which grows from love and which had perhaps been denied to Emma in the last years of their life together were now poured out in poem after poem, the poet attempting to atone through his poetry for what he felt had been the neglect of the man and husband whilst his wife was alive. These poems to Emma's memory were published in the volumes *Satires of Circumstance* (1914) and *Moments of Vision* (1917).

Early in 1914 Hardy married Florence Dugdale. A new round of social activities ensued, with visits to London and Cambridge to see and be seen by friends. This was followed by a journey to Devonshire, a car now replacing the bicycle and pony of earlier years. Six months after their marriage, war was declared and Hardy was invited by the government to join a group of distinguished writers who had banded together to put the case for Britain and her allies before the neutral countries. A number of his wartime poems were probably written with this in mind, but Hardy's faith in the progress of man was sadly shaken by the war and it helped to confirm for him his often expressed belief that there was no 'ultimate wisdom' behind the universe.

Hardy continued to write poetry but, with age, he was becoming frailer. He suffered from various ailments and began to curtail his travelling. He rejected J. M. Barrie's suggestion that he should accompany him to France to see life behind the Lines and he declined an invitation to visit the United States 'after the war'. He did, however, make the journey to Oxford in 1920 to receive an honorary D.Litt. and to watch a performance of *The Dynasts* by the Oxford University Dramatic Society. Another visit to Oxford soon after his eighty-third birthday was his last long journey away from home. After that he never again slept a night away from Max Gate.

Hardy died in January 1928 after a short illness. He was cremated and his ashes were buried in Westminster Abbey, but his heart was carried back to Dorset where it belonged and buried in his first wife's grave in Stinsford churchyard.

Hardy was born three years after Queen Victoria's accession to the throne; he survived her reign and that of her son, Edward VII, as well as the greater part of the reign of George V. During his long life – and he lived through the Crimean War, the Indian Mutiny, the Boer War and the Great War – he was stirred most by the slow, but inexorable movement of social history. He watched the decline of what had been, at least on the surface, a flourishing agricultural economy, but what was of more significance to him, he watched also the decline of the agricultural community.

The Mayor of Casterbridge, though published in 1886, is set back historically in the crucial years before the Repeal of the Corn Law. The year 1815 had marked not only the cessation of hostilities against Napoleon, and the Treaty of Vienna, but also the beginning of an artificially bolstered time of prosperity for the British farmer since the Corn Law of that year imposed heavy duties on the imports of foreign corn. It was not until 1846 that this law was repealed and during that time protection had helped the wealthy landowners to flourish at the expense of the poor and indigent. Meanwhile, the ruthless march of progress was sweeping away the old inefficient, though often kindly paternal business methods, and replacing them by ordered systems; machines were taking the place of men and working more efficiently and more cheaply; men were migrating from the country to the towns; small businesses were giving way to large ones, small farms being absorbed by larger; a limited form of centralisation was bringing to the big towns the trade that for centuries had been carried on in country villages. Nowhere were these changes more apparent than in the rich farming lands of south-west England, the area designated by Hardy as Wessex, after the old kingdom of Wessex in the days before the Norman Conquest, and approximating roughly to the counties of Dorset, Somerset, Wiltshire and Hampshire. Here the changes were in rural living itself for the Industrial Revolution had by-passed Wessex, yet its products were slowly altering the customs and quality of Wessex life.

It is these changes, in the moment of their turn, that Hardy manages to capture. The pages of his novels preserve not only the physical features of the countryside and villages he describes, but also country customs both convivial and cruel, the 'skimmity-ride' being as much part of life as the church choir with their 'bass-viols, fiddles, and flutes' or the principal hiring fair on Old Candlemas Day. Though witchcraft had been prevalent up to the seventeenth century it had dwindled away and in the mid-eighteenth century the Acts against it were removed from the Statute Books; nevertheless its practice was still furtively carried on, and superstition among countryfolk was rife. The Casterbridge 'weather-prophet' lived apart, several miles from the town; no one confessed to believing in him, yet many consulted him 'for a fancy' and paid him well. When a man appeared to be dogged by ill-luck he could easily believe, with Henchard, that someone was sticking pins in a wax image of him, or brewing a magic potion against him. Yet such beliefs were not incompatible with going to church on Sundays, reading the Bible and subscribing to the conventional religious beliefs of the community. At the same time, these religious beliefs were themselves often held in magical awe, so that Michael Henchard could make his vow of abstinence only upon the Bible lying on the church altar, but, by the same token, that vow once made was binding and irrevocable.

Such ideas were perhaps intensified by the very nature of the Wessex countryside with its ancient historical monuments dating back to Neolithic times and the richness of its Roman remains. In *Tess of the D'Urbervilles* Hardy makes use of Stonehenge at the climax of the novel. In *The Mayor of Casterbridge* it is at the Maumbury Ring (itself Neolithic in origin) that Henchard arranges to meet Susan after their long estrangement. These monuments to the distant past, built by men dead and forgotten, may well make human life seem insignificant when viewed in the perspective of time and may well appear to suggest awesome powers.

It is not possible to read Hardy's novels without being impressed by the part Nature plays in men's lives. Though, particularly in the earlier novels, there are idyllic scenes of natural beauty and the regular cycle of the seasons is shown in all its variety, Nature generally seems harsh, and often vindictive. Yet, if it appears to be hostile, it is a hostility which man has imputed to it by purporting to believe in its benevolence. Hardy shows Nature, in fact, as a force indifferent to man. Henchard's ruin was brought about, not by the deliberately malevolent caprices of the weather, but by his own headstrong character. More and more in the later novels Hardy is concerned with the idea contained in the sentence he quotes in Chapter 17 of *The Mayor of Casterbridge*: 'Character is Fate.' It is the first novel in which he explores this theory so fully, the juxtaposition of events in time and place becoming a fatal concord only because of the character of Henchard. There will be further discussion of this in Part 3 of these notes.

The language of *The Mayor of Casterbridge* is not difficult to understand, the main problem arising in the use of dialect and archaic words. In Part 2 it has not seemed necessary to explain words which can be looked up in a good short dictionary, such as *The Concise Oxford Dictionary*, but any difficulties which might not easily be resolved by recourse to a dictionary are explained. More detailed annotations can be found in the New Wessex Edition of the novel.

A note on the text

The Mayor of Casterbridge was begun in 1884 and the first draft was finished in April 1885. After its completion Hardy revised parts of the manuscript in order to include an exciting incident in every instalment of the serial publication. This work was completed by mid-October 1885 and the novel was published simultaneously in weekly instalments in the *Graphic* in Great Britain and in *Harper's Weekly* in the United States. In preparation for book publication he then revised the novel again, this time cutting out various incidents he had put in for the serialised version. The novel was published in two volumes by Smith, Elder and Company in May 1886.

Hardy revised the novel again for a second edition published in one volume in 1887 by Sampson Low.

He made yet another major revision for the uniform edition of his novels published by Osgood, McIlvaine and Company in 1895, of which it was the third volume; he also wrote a preface for this edition.

He made further revisions for the Wessex edition of his works published by Macmillan and Company in 1912. This was for many years the definitive edition of Hardy's works.

He also provided a few minor corrections for the Mellstock edition published by Macmillans in 1920–21. This was the last major edition to be published during Hardy's lifetime.

The text of the New Wessex Edition published by Macmillans in 1974 with an introduction by Ian Gregor and notes by Bryn Caless is based on the Wessex Edition. This is now considered to be the definitive edition of Hardy's works.

Part 2

Summaries
of THE MAYOR OF
CASTERBRIDGE

A general summary

The opening incidents of this novel serve as prologue to the main story: in a mood of stubborn drunkenness Michael Henchard, a young hay-trusser, sells his wife and daughter to a sailor at Weydon-Priors fair. In the sober light of the next day, full of remorse, he tries to find them, but they have vanished without trace. He finally abandons the search but, intent on reforming, he takes a vow of abstinence for twenty-one years. He then makes his way towards the town of Casterbridge.

The main action opens nineteen years later. Henchard has stuck to his vow and by his industry has risen to a position of wealth and influence. Now he is not only a prosperous and flourishing corn-factor but he is also Mayor of Casterbridge. During all these years he has heard nothing of his missing wife and has begun to believe her dead. Thus he has at last felt free to offer the reparation of marriage to a young woman in Jersey with whom he had formed a liaison of a compromising kind at a time when he was ill and desperately lonely.

Susan, however, is not dead. For many years she had believed her union with the sailor, Richard Newson, to be legal. They had left England for Canada almost immediately after the sale. The child, Elizabeth-Jane, died and when Newson's daughter was born she was christened with the same name. They later returned to England where a friend cast doubts upon the legality of Susan's position; therefore, when some time after this the news that Newson was lost at sea was brought to her, she decided to seek out her former husband again, intending, however, to conceal from him the secret of Elizabeth-Jane's birth.

Arrived in Casterbridge, Susan is surprised to discover how Henchard has prospered. This makes her nervous of approaching him and she decides to lodge in Casterbridge overnight. Next day she sends Elizabeth to Henchard with the message that 'Susan Newson, a sailor's widow, is in the town'. He is visibly moved to hear that Susan is still alive, but is pleased to realise that the girl knows nothing of their past relationship. Determined on making amends to Susan, he arranges to meet her that evening at the old Roman Amphitheatre known as the Ring. At this meeting, he suggests that she should come to live in Casterbridge and that, in the course of time, he should court her and marry her again, thus keeping his past folly secret.

By coincidence, the very day on which Susan had arrived in Casterbridge marked also the arrival of someone else who was to play a major part in Michael Henchard's story. This was Donald Farfrae, an engaging young Scotsman, who was passing through the town on his way to Bristol and from there to America. He too stays overnight. By a stroke of luck he is able to do a good turn for Henchard who, attracted by the young man's joyful and lively personality, persuades him to remain in Casterbridge and become the manager of his business, although this post had been all but finally offered to another man, Joshua Jopp. Although he hardly knows him, Henchard finds himself confiding his strange story to Farfrae; he tells him not only of Susan's return, but also of his, Henchard's, involvement with the young woman in Jersey. He asks Farfrae to help him write a letter of explanation to this young woman and with the letter he encloses a cheque, intending that this incident of his life shall be closed.

Henchard's plans to make amends to his wife progress smoothly; the wedding takes place and Susan and Elizabeth move from their small cottage to the Mayor's house. For a while both are happy there. In her new-found wealth and security Elizabeth blossoms and Henchard, believing her to be his own daughter, becomes greatly attached to her; however, when he proposes that she should change her name to Henchard, Susan opposes the suggestion.

It is soon apparent, too, that Farfrae is attracted to Elizabeth, but before this friendship comes to fruition differences begin to arise between him and Henchard. During his short stay in Casterbridge Farfrae's even temper and cheerful and open manner have made him a popular figure in the town. He has reorganised Henchard's business and, though unwittingly, he is gradually ousting him from his position as the most admired and respected man in Casterbridge. Henchard finds himself becoming jealous of his manager and two incidents serve to bring his anger to a head: first, Farfrae defies him when he treats one of his workmen, Abel Whittle, roughly and foolishly; secondly, when both men organise a local celebration, Farfrae's turns out to be the more successful. In a moment of hasty temper, Henchard dismisses his able young manager, who then decides to set up in the corn business for himself. When Henchard hears this he forbids him to see Elizabeth again.

After a while Susan is taken ill. She is clearly dying and one day, with what little strength she has left, she writes a letter to her husband, directing him not to open it until Elizabeth-Jane's wedding-day; she locks this letter in her desk. She lingers for some days and then dies. Henchard now feels he wants to reclaim his daughter as his own and he tells her enough of his early story to convince her that he is her father, although he stops short at telling her about the sale at Weydon-Priors fair. Searching for evidence of his story he comes across Susan's last letter and, finding it not to be properly sealed, he takes it out and reads it. It is the most bitter moment of his life, for the letter tells him the truth about Elizabeth's birth and thus at the moment of his reclaiming her he has lost her forever. His misery and anger at the ironic sequence of events persuades him to stick to his story and not tell Elizabeth the new truth he has discovered. However, the thought that she is really Newson's daughter turns his love to bitterness and hate. Elizabeth is astonished and deeply distressed when she realises that Henchard no longer cares for her.

Meanwhile, during his wife's illness, Henchard had received a letter from Lucetta, the young woman from Jersey, asking him to return all the letters she had ever written to him. She sets a time when she will be passing through Casterbridge on the coach and asks him to deliver the letters to her at the coach office. He keeps the appointment, but she is not there. She has, in fact, been prevented from keeping the appointment by the death of her aunt, from whom she inherits a substantial fortune. When she hears that Susan Henchard has also died she decides to take her aunt's name, Templeman, and move to Casterbridge, hoping that Henchard will now make amends to her in her turn. To this end she takes the tenancy of High-Place Hall, a stone mansion of character overlooking the market-place.

Chancing to meet Elizabeth soon after her arrival, and learning that she is unhappy, Lucetta invites the girl to live with her as her companion. She then writes to Henchard, telling him of her presence in Casterbridge. When he tries to see her, however, she sends him a message asking him to return the next day and in his obstinacy he resolves not to repeat his visit for a while. After three days Lucetta sends Elizabeth out for the morning and again writes to Henchard asking him to come to see her. Then she sits and waits, but when a visitor arrives it is Farfrae, not Henchard. He has come to visit Elizabeth in response to a note from her stepfather giving him permission to resume his courtship of her. When he is confronted with Lucetta he stays and talks to her and they find themselves strongly attracted to each other. Elizabeth watches in anguish as the affair between the two progresses. Farfrae does not know that Lucetta is the other woman in Henchard's story, and the latter finds himself rebuffed, but is not certain of the identity of his rival.

Now Henchard determines to outdo Farfrae in business. He takes on as his manager Joshua Jopp, whom he had earlier rejected, and plans to ruin the younger man by a massive buying and selling of corn. He is too rash, however, and manages only to ruin himself, whereas Farfrae, by more judicious trade, has prospered. Henchard dismisses Jopp in anger. He then decides to settle matters finally with Lucetta, but by chance he overhears Farfrae proposing to her. When Farfrae has left her

Henchard visits her and forces her to agree to marry him by threatening to disclose their earlier intimacy.

It is at this moment that Henchard's past catches up with him again. Though no longer Mayor he is still a magistrate and the next day the old furmity-woman from Weydon-Priors is brought before him. Recognising him, she denounces him and in shame he leaves the court-room. As soon as Lucetta hears the story she decides that she can never marry such a man; she now arranges to go to Port-Bredy with Farfrae and marry him secretly. When he hears of the marriage Henchard is bitterly angry. Elizabeth, to whom Lucetta had earlier told her own story using assumed names, now realises the identities of all the people concerned and in deep distress she leaves High-Place Hall and takes lodgings close to her stepfather's house.

Soon after this Henchard's personal and business misfortunes result in his bankruptcy. He goes to live in Jopp's cottage and Farfrae buys both his house and business. The younger man attempts a reconciliation with his former patron, but his efforts are rejected, and Henchard takes a job as journeyman hay-trusser in the yard where he had until lately been master. It is now rumoured in the town that Farfrae is to be proposed as Mayor and this revives Henchard's hatred of him. The twenty-one years of abstinence are almost at an end and when Henchard is at last released from his vow he turns to drink to console himself for the ills that have befallen him. Drink and hatred now make him look for the means of revenging himself upon Farfrae, especially as the sudden death of the Mayor precipitates the young Scotsman into the Mayoralty.

It is Lucetta who gives him his first chance of revenge. One day in the market she renews her request for the return of her letters. He remembers that the bundle is in the wall-safe of his old house, the very house now occupied by Lucetta and her husband. That evening he goes to the house and asks Farfrae if he can retrieve the letters. He then sits and reads them to the young man, but cannot bring himself to act so meanly as to read the signature, so he finally leaves with the letters still in his possession. At a further request for their return he entrusts them to Jopp who promises to deliver them. Jopp, however, has a grudge against most of the principals in the story and, on a visit to Peter's Finger, a low-class inn, he is easily persuaded to undo the bundle and read the letters aloud before delivering them. When the patrons of Peter's Finger hear of the affair between Henchard and Lucetta they decide to punish them by the country custom of arranging a skimmity-ride in which effigies of the two offenders are tied back to back on a donkey and paraded through the streets accompanied by the noise of a primitive band.

Whilst plans for the skimmity-ride are going ahead in the poorer part of the town, more official celebrations are in hand to welcome a royal visitor who is going to pass through Casterbridge. Farfrae, now Mayor, is to read a loyal address, and the people of the town gather in all their finery to pay homage to their visitor. At the crucial moment, however, it is Henchard, half-drunk, in old and dirty clothes, who steps forward first. Farfrae swiftly pushes him aside and the rest of the brief visit passes off well, but Henchard is now determined to settle with his rival once and for all. He arranges to meet Farfrae in the granaries where he intends to fight him to the death. Being the stronger man he ties one of his hands behind his back, yet even with his one hand he soon has Farfrae in a position where he will fall from a trap-door and kill himself. At the last moment, however, Henchard cannot bring himself to kill his one-time friend. He allows Farfrae to leave and hears him say in the yard below that he has to go to Weatherbury.

Later that day the skimmity-ride takes place and Lucetta, seeing the effigies of Henchard and herself, overcome with shame, and fearing that Farfrae will discover the truth, falls in a fit and dies before morning.

The next day Henchard's peace is further disturbed by the arrival at his house of Richard Newson, who is alive after all. Henchard, in a moment of rash panic, tells him that both Susan and Elizabeth are dead and to his astonishment the sailor leaves the town without further question. Now a brief period of tranquillity begins for Henchard, haunted always by the belief that Newson will return. The ex-corn merchant takes over a small seed-shop and Elizabeth goes to live with him. Time passes; Farfrae renews his attentions to Elizabeth and at last their wedding is arranged. Suddenly Newson returns and, rather than face his step-daughter's knowledge of the truth, Henchard leaves the town to become an itinerant hay-trusser once again.

When Elizabeth-Jane hears that she is really Newson's daughter after all she feels that she can never forgive her stepfather for deceiving her. However, on her wedding-day he returns to see her, bringing her a present of a caged song-bird and hoping for reconciliation. She thoughtlessly rebuffs him and he leaves, a broken man. He is followed by one of his old workmen, Abel Whittle, who feels sorry for him. Some weeks later the song-bird is found dead under a bush in Farfrae's garden and Elizabeth-Jane is distressed when she remembers how harshly she had turned Henchard away. She and Farfrae now scour the surrounding countryside looking for him, but when they find him it is just too late, for despite Whittle's attempts to help him he has died in misery and bitterness.

Detailed summaries

Chapter 1

A young man and woman are trudging towards the village of Weydon-Priors on a late summer evening. The woman carries a small girl. The man is identified as a hay-trusser by the clothes he is wearing and the tools he is carrying. The two preserve an absolute silence between them. When they reach the village it turns out to be Fair Day and, tired, they look for refreshment. The woman persuades her husband not to go into the tent where beer and cider are sold, but to enter the furmity tent instead. She soon realises her mistake, for the furmity is being laced with illicit rum and her husband is very quickly the worse for drink.

There is a dramatic shift in tone as the young man, half-drunk, decides to auction his wife; it is a bizarre auction, with the price rising though no one makes a bid until it reaches five guineas when a sailor offers to pay that sum. The bargain is struck; the sailor pays five new Bank of England pound notes and five shillings; then he departs with the woman and the child, Elizabeth-Jane. As she leaves, the woman throws her wedding ring across the tent. The crowd drifts away and the hay-trusser drops into a drunken sleep.

This opening chapter establishes the time of the action and introduces the man who is to dominate the rest of the book. As yet unnamed, he is by no means an attractive character: surly, drunken, impetuous, he appears to deserve to lose his wife and child. The fourth paragraph, which describes the young woman, suggests the importance of the roles which Nature and man respectively are to play in the novel. Towards the end of the chapter, after the sale, Hardy picks up this theme again, philosophising on the cosmic significance of his themes.

NOTES AND GLOSSARY:
(Throughout these notes 'dial' indicates dialect)

nater:	*(dial)* nature
hay-trusser:	one who cuts hay and secures it in bundles or 'trusses'
furmity:	a healthy country drink made from wheat grain, raisins and spices boiled in milk
brood-mare:	a mare kept for breeding
chiel:	*(dial)* child
staylace dealer:	one who sells laces for tightening corsets or 'stays'
guinea:	one pound and one shilling in old money; now 105 new pence
'pon my 'vation:	*(dial)* a mild oath meaning 'upon my salvation'
clane:	*(dial)* clean

keacorn: *(dial)* throat
the great trumpet: a reference to the Day of Judgement when the trumpets will sound. See Isaiah 27:13

Chapter 2

The next morning when the young man awakes the furmity-tent is deserted, but his hazy memories of the happenings of the previous night are confirmed by the discovery of his wife's wedding-ring lying on the floor amidst the rubble and by the bank-notes in his pocket. He decides that he had not revealed his identity to anyone and he quickly leaves the tent and the district. When he reaches the next village he enters the church and makes a solemn vow to God that for twenty-one years he will give up all strong drink. It is during the making of this vow that we learn that the man's name is Michael Henchard. He now sets out to search for his wife and daughter, but though he is forced to spend the sailor's money on his search, all is in vain. After months of fruitless wandering he arrives in a seaport and is told that people fitting his description of his wife and daughter and the sailor had recently emigrated. Henchard then gives up the search and makes for the town of Casterbridge.

Here we see another side of Henchard, serious, proud, ashamed of his previous behaviour and anxious to make amends; yet the impetuous sale of the evening before is recalled by his impetuous vow to abstain from strong drink. A typical Hardyesque scene is presented to us when Henchard looks out of the furmity-tent and sees before him the present-day scene with its hills and valleys marked with both the forts and barrows of prehistoric men and the gay vans of the gipsies and showmen.

NOTES AND GLOSSARY:
the Seven . . . dog: the Seven Sleepers of Ephesus were Christian youths who fled from persecution in AD250 and slept for 300 years. Their dog, Katmir, went with them and stood by them during their long sleep
foot-pace: the place before the altar where the priest stands to offer the sacrament

Chapter 3

Many years later the highroad to Weydon-Priors is again being traversed on Fair Day by Susan, the woman who had been sold. She now calls herself Mrs Newson and she is accompanied by her grown-up daughter, Elizabeth-Jane. Both women are in mourning for the sailor, Richard Newson, who has been lost at sea. When they enter the fairground Susan sees the furmity-seller, now a wretched, wrinkled hag, selling her furmity in the open. From her she learns that Michael Henchard moved to Casterbridge many years ago.

The time-shift is emphasised to us not only by the changes in the human participants in the story, but also by the changes in the scene at the Fair itself where country business is dwindling. Hardy's ironic purpose depends upon the reader realizing that, with the passing of the years, the furmity-woman has almost forgotten the sale of Susan Henchard. She was reminded of it first by Michael Henchard himself a year after the sale and now Susan calls it back to her mind once more.

Chapter 4

By means of a brief flashback Hardy fills in a little of Susan's history. She had lived with Newson for many years, first in Canada and then back in England at Falmouth, until she was made to doubt the validity of her union with him. Not long after she confided this to him, Newson was apparently lost at sea on his next voyage. Susan had then decided to set out with Elizabeth to find her real husband again. When they arrive in Casterbridge they find that the people are angry because their bread is being made from overgrown wheat which makes the loaves indigestible.

Our first introduction to Casterbridge itself is through Elizabeth's eyes: the town is enclosed, boxed in by trees, as the two women are later to be confined and boxed in by their Casterbridge life. Hardy's interest in architecture is apparent in his description of the High Street houses and of the church, his interest in country life by the detailed observations of the goods for sale in the Casterbridge shops.

NOTES AND GLOSSARY:

brick-nogging: timber framework filled with bricks

field-flagons: containers designed to be filled with ale, beer or cider and taken to work by field-labourers

seed-lip: a kind of bowl in which a sower carried the seed for scattering on the fields

Sicilian Mariners' Hymn: this is a well-known setting of the nineteenth Psalm. The chimes would probably play the opening bars

swipes: *(slang)* small beer

corn-factor: one who buys and sells corn as a business; a corn merchant

growed wheat: *(dial)* wheat which has begun to sprout before it has been harvested

blowed bladders: pigs' bladders were often cleaned and blown up as balls

Chapter 5

The sound of band music attracts Susan and her daughter to the King's Arms, the chief hotel in Casterbridge, where many people are gathered together inside and out. A big public dinner is going on with the Mayor in the chair. To Susan's discomfort, the Mayor is Michael Henchard, now a flourishing corn merchant. Whilst talking to some labourers in the crowd Elizabeth learns of Henchard's vow of abstinence and is told that it has two more years to run. As the dinner continues, Henchard, who is telling stories to the guests, is interrupted by some of the small tradesmen and criticised for the bad wheat he has been selling.

The contrast between Michael Henchard's present state of affluence and his position at the beginning of the book is emphasised by Susan's memory of him then. Yet, though he is now seen to be sober and prosperous, Hardy shows us the passion smouldering just below the surface. However, his men speak well of him and he keeps his temper under strict control. The passage of time is established through the reference to the vow and we realise that nineteen years have passed; we should remind ourselves that in Chapter 3 Hardy described Elizabeth-Jane as 'a well-formed young woman about eighteen'; this apparent discrepancy is vital to the plot.

NOTES AND GLOSSARY:

portico:	entrance
fall:	veil
akin to a coach:	related to the owner of a horse and carriage
as stern . . . Jews:	a reference to God's anger when the Jews made and worshipped a golden calf; see Exodus 32
list:	*(dial)* hard layer of unrisen dough

Chapter 6

A young man overhears the discussion about Henchard's corn and writes the Mayor a note. He then decides to stay the night at the Three Mariners Inn. Elizabeth and her mother also go there and, soon after, Henchard follows to seek out the young man.

The reader's first impression of Donald Farfrae is of a pleasant and personable young man; yet he clearly has a tinge of Henchard's impulsiveness in his nature.

NOTES AND GLOSSARY:

ruddy . . . countenance:	'David . . . was but a youth, and ruddy, and of a fair countenance.' 1 Samuel 17: 42
yard of clay:	long-stemmed clay pipe for smoking tobacco

Chapter 7

Elizabeth and Susan take lodgings at the Three Mariners and there they overhear Farfrae telling Henchard how to restore his bad wheat to an eatable condition. The Mayor is so pleased and touched by Farfrae's help that he tries to persuade the young man to take a job with him as corn-factor's manager. Farfrae refuses, however, insisting that he intends to emigrate to America.

This chapter contains several of Hardy's favourite narrative devices: the intruder from outside whose superior knowledge and new ideas are to effect changes in the town and contribute to catastrophe; the opportunity missed in the chance encounter between Farfrae and Elizabeth-Jane when she carries up his supper; and Elizabeth's offer to help in the inn, which action later brings Henchard's wrath upon her.

NOTES AND GLOSSARY:

twelve-bushel strength:	the strength of beer was reckoned by the amount of malt added to a barrel. The Three Mariners sold strong beer
Farfrae:	frae far in Scots dialect: from afar
dog days:	the hottest time of the year when the Dog Star is in the ascendancy
to the pitching:	until it is empty

Chapter 8

After Henchard has left, Farfrae joins the company downstairs and is persuaded to sing some of his native songs. He does so with such feeling that everyone is moved and Elizabeth feels a lively sympathy with him. Meanwhile, from outside, Henchard has heard the songs and feels strangely drawn towards the young man.

The story progresses little in this chapter, but the magnetism of Farfrae is established; he immediately becomes a dominant personality, winning the admiration of the comic chorus of country men, of Elizabeth-Jane, of Henchard and of everyone else who hears him.

NOTES AND GLOSSARY:

lammigers:	*(dial)* cripples
cust:	*(dial)* cursed
wounded:	*(dial)* infatuated
bruckle:	*(dial)* rough and ready
chine:	the projecting rim of a barrel
gaberlunzie:	*(Scots dial)* wandering beggar
toss-pots:	*(archaic)* drunkards

Chapter 9

Next morning Henchard passes the inn and offers to accompany Farfrae
to the edge of the town. Later, Susan sends her daughter to Henchard
with a message. Elizabeth makes her way to the Mayor's house and is
surprised to find Farfrae there. Hardy goes on to explain how this had
come about.

In this chapter Casterbridge is shown as a market town closely
connected with rural life. Market day in Casterbridge is important to the
whole movement of the novel and here the bustling atmosphere and
busy life which is Henchard's background, and is to be that of Farfrae, is
established.

NOTES AND GLOSSARY:

bloody warriors: *(dial)* wallflowers

chassez-déchassez *(French)* a dancing step in which the dancer moves
sideways, then back again

Terpsichorean: Terpsichore is the Muse of dancing

Cranstoun's Goblin Page: Lord Cranstoun's dwarf, a cruel practical
joker, in Sir Walter Scott's poem *The Lay of the Last
Minstrel*

staddles: supports to raise the floor off the ground

Chapter 10

Whilst Elizabeth waits, Joshua Jopp, who had expected to be appointed
as Henchard's manager, comes in, but he is told that the post is filled;
Elizabeth observes how this news angers and disappoints him. She now
gives Henchard her message and, visibly moved, he writes a note to
Susan, asking her to meet him that evening at the Casterbridge Ring;
with it he encloses five guineas, thus making symbolic repayment of her
purchase money to her.

A favourite device of Hardy's is, as here, unexpectedly to confront a
character with someone from the past. Henchard comes through the
ordeal well and we are impressed by his desire to make amends.

NOTES AND GLOSSARY:

The quicker . . .Bethesda: the pool of Bethesda in Jerusalem had healing
powers for the first sick person to enter it after an
angel had touched the waters. St John 5: 1-9 tells the
story of the crippled man who had waited for many
years to be healed but was always too slow to enter
the pool first

rouge-et-noir: *(French)* red and black

Chapter 11

The Roman Amphitheatre at Casterbridge, known as the Ring, is described and an atmosphere of desolation and superstitious fear is evoked. Here Michael Henchard meets his one-time wife. He proposes a plan by which he may court her again, re-marry her and adopt Elizabeth as his step-daughter, thereby keeping his past disgrace a secret.

By a subtle shift of emphasis from the characters to the geographical location, Hardy places his story in a cosmic perspective. The problems of Michael and Susan Henchard are seen against the vast and ancient background of the Amphitheatre with its knowledge of life and death.

NOTES AND GLOSSARY:

Jötuns: mythological giants in Scandinavian folklore

Chapter 12

When he returns from seeing Susan, Henchard persuades Farfrae to go back home with him and as they sit together by the fire he feels drawn to tell the young man the story of his marriage and parting from Susan; he also reveals that he had promised to marry a young woman who lives in Jersey. However, having decided that he must make amends to Susan, he asks Farfrae to help him draft a letter to the second woman. He encloses a cheque with the letter, feeling that this at least will make some slight reparation to the young woman.

The story progresses swiftly in this chapter as the complication of the second woman is introduced. We are again reminded of Henchard's impulsiveness by the naïve way in which he unfolds the whole burden of his past life to a young man he hardly knows and yet feels attracted to.

NOTES AND GLOSSARY:

education of Achilles: the Greek mythological hero, Achilles, was educated as a hunter and fighter

Laocoöns: in Greek legend the priest Laocoön and his sons were crushed to death by serpents

Job ... birth: 'Let the day perish wherein I was born, and the night in which it was said, There is a man child conceived.' The Book of Job 3:3.

Chapter 13

In pursuance of his plan Henchard establishes Susan comfortably in a cottage and, after sufficient time has elapsed, he marries her. The marriage is the occasion of idle gossip and joking among the labouring community, but it is all quite good-humoured.

Here, Hardy again returns to the ancient past of Casterbridge and its surroundings, yet he emphasises not only the serenity, but also the melancholy of a 'past-marked prospect'. It chimes in well with our view of Susan at this time, for although she is genteelly settled, such epithets as 'poor', 'fragile', 'pale', 'humble' are constantly used to describe her.

NOTES AND GLOSSARY:

twanking:	*(dial)* complaining
pair of jumps:	*(dial)* a woman's bodice or vest
night-rail:	*(dial)* a night-dress

Chapter 14

Susan settles comfortably as Mrs Henchard again and Elizabeth is delighted to live in pleasant, affluent surroundings; despite their new-found comfort, however, Susan is reluctant to allow Elizabeth's name to be changed to Henchard. One day a mysterious message results in a meeting between Elizabeth and Farfrae in an empty granary, but they do not discover who has arranged the meeting and they soon part.

The modest, careful, temperate character of Elizabeth-Jane is here contrasted with the much more forceful and impulsive character of Henchard. This contrast is emphasised in the very chapter in which Hardy builds up a sense of mystery around the two women.

NOTES AND GLOSSARY:

puffings: fancy clothes with lavish puffed sleeves and frills

Chapter 15

After the warmth of their early friendship disagreements begin to arise between Henchard and Farfrae. The original cause is Henchard's harsh treatment of one of his workmen, Abel Whittle, but the more deep-rooted reason is that Henchard finds himself diminished in the eyes of his fellow townsmen when he is compared with Farfrae. Though their friendship continues, it is blighted.

Once more it is Henchard's impetuous nature that gets him into difficulties, but this time he is opposed by a firmness and determination in Farfrae that has not been seen before; the brief moments of tension between the two men result in mastery for Farfrae.

NOTES AND GLOSSARY:

scrags: *(dial)* bits

the prophet . . . go gay:	'And taking gold, as it were for a virgin that loveth to go gay, they make crowns for the heads of their gods.' The Apocrypha, Baruch 6:9
moment-hand:	second hand of a watch or clock
chap o' wax:	one who is rising (like the waxing moon)

Chapter 16

The friendship between Henchard and Farfrae cools gradually; both arrange festivities to celebrate a day of national rejoicing, Henchard lavishly, in the open air, and free, Farfrae more modestly, under cover, and charging for admission. But Henchard has reckoned without the weather and the rain washes out his festivities. Farfrae's are more successful, however, and cause the townsfolk to say that in every way the manager does better than his master. Angered at such statements, Henchard announces that Farfrae is about to leave him and the Scotsman decides to take him at his word.

The ironies of character and Fate now begin to combine to push Henchard downwards: Farfrae, whom he has raised, now begins to outshine him and Nature joins in with inopportune weather to defeat his plans. Yet Henchard's impulses are to some extent good and generous; his celebrations are prepared with an open heart and an open hand; we cannot feel that he really deserves the crushing blows which now begin to fall on him.

NOTES AND GLOSSARY:

Correggio:	an Italian painter (1494–1534)
stunpoll:	*(dial)* stupid fellow
chaw:	*(dial)* chew (he would chew it to see if it was tender)
randy:	*(dial)* merry-making

Chapter 17

After the festivities Farfrae walks home with Elizabeth and is almost tempted to propose to her. He does not do so, however, and the opportunity is lost, for when he leaves Henchard's employment to set up on his own, his former master forbids him to see Elizabeth again. The antagonism between the two former friends gradually grows.

NOTES AND GLOSSARY:

Jacob in Padan-Aram:	Jacob agreed to work for his father-in-law, Laban, and to receive as wages all the ring-straked and spotted cattle; from that time the ring-straked and spotted cattle prospered; see Genesis 30:25–43

varden:	*(dial)* farthing; this was one quarter of an old penny
sniff and snaff:	popular terms for making an agreement, 'sniff' answered by 'snaff'
Bellerophon:	a Homeric hero who angered the gods and was left to wander lonely and grief-stricken in uninhabited places

Chapter 18

This chapter is much concerned with letters. The first is from Lucetta, the young woman from Jersey, who asks Henchard to return all her old letters to her as she passes through Casterbridge on a certain day. She fails to keep the appointment, however, and Henchard returns home with the packet of old letters. Susan, who has been taken ill, writes a letter to her husband, but she seals it and locks it in her desk, directing that he shall not open it until Elizabeth's wedding-day. She also confesses to her daughter that she had been responsible for sending the notes which caused Farfrae and Elizabeth to meet in the empty granary. Shortly after this confession she dies.

Fate is here seen directing affairs, as Henchard, reminded again of Lucetta, decides that he must marry her if Susan dies, at the very time when Susan is, in fact, dying. Hardy is a master of pathos and the last paragraph of this chapter is a moving comment on the indignities death heaps on life.

NOTES AND GLOSSARY:

ounce pennies:	privately minted coins used for trade purposes; they were generally heavier than coins of the realm issued by the Royal Mint
doxology:	he means 'theology'

Chapter 19

Now that his wife is dead and Farfrae estranged from him, Henchard longs for some human being to love; he decides to tell Elizabeth what he believes to be the truth, that she is his daughter, not Newson's. While doing so he also persuades her to change her name to Henchard. When he searches for proofs to offer her he finds the letter that Susan wrote when she was dying. The seal has come undone and he takes it out and reads it. The letter tells him that his own Elizabeth-Jane is dead and the girl in his house is Newson's daughter. In the shock and anguish of this discovery he wanders out and finds himself in that part of the town which houses the prison; there he sees the gallows, stark and fearful, standing out in the darkness. When he returns home he determines not to tell Elizabeth the truth; the girl herself has accepted the situation, but the kiss she receives from her new father is without warmth.

Not only does Fate continue to rain blows upon Henchard, but also one of Time's ironies is here seen to destroy his peace at the moment he appears to have found it again.

NOTES AND GLOSSARY:

the brethren . . . Joseph: 'Joseph said unto his brethren, I am Joseph; doth my father yet live? And his brethren could not answer him; for they were troubled at his presence.' Genesis 45:3

Prester John: a legendary figure of great wealth. In *Orlando Furioso* Ariosto relates how Prester John attempted to add Paradise to his possessions. The gods punished him for his presumption by setting a table of rich food constantly before him; the food was snatched away by harpies whenever he tried to eat, so that he starved to death. Ludovico Ariosto (1474–1533) the Italian poet, wrote *Orlando Furioso* (1516) to deal with the wars of Charlemagne with the Saracens

Schwarzwasser: *(German)* black water

Chapter 20

As time goes on Henchard can hardly bear the sight of Elizabeth; he constantly criticises her speech, her writing and her habits until she begins to find life a burden to her. One day, overcome with grief, she is sitting beside her mother's grave when a pretty, expensively dressed lady befriends her and suggests an escape from her misery by inviting her to become the lady's companion. Meanwhile, Henchard, anxious to rid himself of the burden of Newson's daughter, writes to Farfrae giving him permission to resume his courtship.

Sympathy for Elizabeth is here mingled with pity for Henchard's anguish. With the introduction of the strange lady the element of mystery in the plot thickens.

NOTES AND GLOSSARY:

Minerva: the Roman goddess of wisdom. She became identified with Athena, the Greek goddess of wisdom and strength and thus the patroness of masculine women

Karnac: the ruined ancient Egyptian city of Thebes on the upper Nile

Princess Ida:	see *The Princess* by Lord Tennyson (1809–92). Elizabeth does not write in an elegant 'lady's hand', but in a masculine fashion. The lines quoted from *The Princess* (1847) refer, in fact, to the writing of one of Princess Ida's suitors who wrote in an assumed hand
Austerlitz:	the battle of Austerlitz (1805) marked the turning point in Napoleon's fortunes
leery:	*(dial)* hungry, weak

Chapter 21

Elizabeth goes secretly to look at High-Place Hall where she hopes to live as the lady's companion. Going quietly out of a little used door at the back of the courtyard she narrowly misses Henchard who is entering the Hall through this doorway. A day or so later she completes her arrangements to go to Miss Templeman's and that evening she leaves Henchard's house.

A sense of anticipation and of intrigue is aroused by the hidden door and the secret visits of both Elizabeth and Henchard to High-Place Hall.

NOTES AND GLOSSARY:

passenger:	used in its old sense of 'a passer-by'

Chapter 22

The story moves back to the night preceding the events of the previous chapter. Henchard receives a letter from Lucetta which informs him that she has come to live in High-Place Hall. After some initial bewilderment he realises that Miss Templeman is Lucetta Le Sueur, by which name he had known Lucetta in Jersey. When she is settled and Elizabeth has gone to her, Lucetta sends another letter to Henchard asking him to visit her, but when he does so she refuses to see him until the next day. As a result, in a mood of obstinacy, he decides to postpone his visit for a few days. When, after several days, he has not arrived, Lucetta sends Elizabeth out and then writes to Henchard again asking him to come to see her. She is awaiting his arrival when another visitor is shown in.

The extravagance of Lucetta's letter-writing is once more apparent and must arouse fear for someone so careless of compromising her situation as to be constantly offering written proof of her thoughts and intentions; a somewhat heedless and foolish character is suggested.

NOTES AND GLOSSARY:

cyma-recta:	an architectural term meaning that the moulding of a cornice has the concave curve uppermost

étourderie: *(French)* thoughtlessness

'Thy speech bewrayeth thee!': 'They that stood by . . . said to Peter, Surely thou also art one of them; for thy speech bewrayeth thee.' St Matthew 26:73

carrefour: *(French)* crossroads

Chapter 23

Lucetta's unexpected visitor is Donald Farfrae who has come to visit Elizabeth-Jane. Lucetta is immediately attracted to him and by telling him that Elizabeth will be back shortly she persuades him to wait. Together they look out over the fair and their talk turns to nostalgic thoughts of their own homes. In this slightly sentimental mood Farfrae saves two lovers from being parted by hiring a young man together with his aged and not very active father. It is a rather uncharacteristic act on his part and this together with their thoughts of home and the past, stirs deep emotions in Lucetta and Farfrae. The young man leaves and when Henchard arrives, Lucetta sends a message that she cannot see him.

A double ironic twist is brought into the story here. Farfrae's arrival at High-Place Hall not only takes his thoughts away from Elizabeth, it also takes Lucetta's thoughts away from Henchard. We see here the Farfrae whose sentimental songs won the hearts of the customers in the Three Mariners when he first arrived in Casterbridge; at the same time we see the hard-headed business man who is well on his way to ousting Michael Henchard from his position. The kind of impetuousness which made Lucetta invite Elizabeth to her home is seen again in her swift emotional response to Farfrae.

Chapter 24

Time passes and each week both Elizabeth and Lucetta wait for Saturday to come, since that day brings Farfrae to the market-place beneath their window. One Saturday a huge agricultural machine arrives there and the two women go out to look at it. They encounter first Henchard and then Farfrae; in this second meeting Elizabeth senses an attraction between Lucetta and Farfrae. A few days later Lucetta tells Elizabeth the story of her connection with Henchard and her love for Farfrae, but she conceals the identities of the people concerned. Although she does not know who the men in the story are, Elizabeth guesses that it is Lucetta's own story.

The horse-drill, imported by Farfrae, symbolises the mechanisation of farming which was taking place. It is identified with Farfrae who is representative of the new business methods, as opposed to Henchard who represents the old country ways.

NOTES AND GLOSSARY:
some falls . . . among thorns: this is a reference to Christ's parable of the sower and the seed; see St Matthew 13:3–7
He that observeth . . . not sow: 'He that observeth the wind shall not sow'. Ecclesiastes 11: 4

Chapter 25

Farfrae begins a sedate courtship of Lucetta and, seeing them together, Elizabeth realises the identities both of the young lady and of the second lover in Lucetta's story. Henchard too persists in his courtship and offers Lucetta marriage, but she rebuffs him. Meanwhile, Elizabeth finds that both men are ardent in their love for her friend, but that they have little affection to spare for her. This loss she endures in silence.

In his love for Lucetta, Farfrae shows a callous indifference to Elizabeth, whilst she exhibits a vast capacity for passive suffering.

NOTES AND GLOSSARY:
Protean variety: Proteus, the old man of the sea from Greek mythology, was able to change shape at will.
'meaner beauties of the night': a reference to the stars; the quotation is from 'On His Mistress the Queen of Bohemia' by Sir Henry Wotton (1568–1639)

Chapter 26

Henchard begins to suspect that Farfrae is his rival in love and decides to ruin his business and drive him from the town. To help him he engages Joshua Jopp, whom he had previously rejected, as his foreman. Being a superstitious man at heart, however, he goes to consult the local weather prophet and is told that the harvest weather will be wet and stormy. He then decides to buy up large stocks of grain which he hopes to sell later at a profit. When he has bought as much as he possibly can the weather changes and a good harvest looks certain after all. Henchard now has to sell at a loss and he blames Jopp for not advising him against his course; he then dismisses Jopp, who vows vengeance.

Henchard's rashness once more causes trouble for him and his impetuous dismissal of Jopp gains him an enemy. Hardy's interest in country-lore is shown here in the story of the weather-prophet.

NOTES AND GLOSSARY:
Tuscan painting: a painting of the Florentine school, which comprised a group of painters of the early Renaissance
dungmixen: *(dial)* dung-hill

two disciples . . . Emmaus:	'Two of them went that same day to a village called Emmaus . . . and . . . he sat at meat with them . . . and their eyes were opened and they knew him.' St Luke 24:29–30
Saul . . . Samuel:	'Saul drew near to Samuel in the gate, and said Tell me, I pray thee, where the seer's house is, And Samuel answered Saul, and said, I am the seer: go up before me unto the high place; for ye shall eat with me today . . .' 1 Samuel 9:18–19
toad-bag:	a charm prepared by wizards, consisting of toads' legs in a little bag

Chapter 27

The harvest has hardly begun when the weather breaks and proves the weather-prophet right after all. Although Henchard's rash transactions have lost him a great deal of money, Farfrae's more modest trading has made him a profit. Rivalry between the two grows both in business and in love. After Henchard overhears a lover's conversation between Lucetta and Farfrae, he visits Lucetta and, by threatening disclosure of their affair in Jersey, he forces her to agree to marry him. Elizabeth-Jane is called as witness of her promise.

Whilst good fortune seems to be on Farfrae's side, Henchard appears to be dogged by misfortune. This makes him heartless towards Lucetta and his impetuosity is again demonstrated when he wrings a promise of marriage from her. The reader is being prepared for her illness and death later in the book by her fainting after making her promise and by Elizabeth's comment that she is unable to bear much.

NOTES AND GLOSSARY:

to follow . . . Capitol:	in Roman times defeated leaders were forced to follow the victorious general in a triumphal procession to the Capitol Hill in Rome
zwailing along:	*(dial)* wandering aimlessly
gawk-hammer:	*(dial)* stupid
thill horse:	the last of a team of shaft horses
giddying worm:	a parasitic worm which, eaten by sheep, causes giddiness and death
flagrant:	he means 'vagrant'

Chapter 28

In the absence of the Mayor for the year, Henchard presides at the magistrates' Court. There he is confronted with the old furmity-seller from Weydon Fair, who is being tried for disorderly conduct. She reveals the story of how he sold his wife and, declining to give judgement on her, he vacates the magistrates' bench. After hearing this story Lucetta is greatly disturbed and leaves home to have a few days' rest in the seaside town of Port-Bredy. Several days later Henchard calls on her only to learn that although she has returned home she has gone for a walk along the Port-Bredy road.

- Fate now seems to rain blow after blow upon Henchard. The furmity-woman's disclosure seems cruelly unfair on a man who has tried so hard to redeem himself. The reappearance of a figure from the past who reveals a carefully guarded secret is one of Hardy's favourite narrative devices.

NOTES AND GLOSSARY:

Shallow and Silence: country justices from Shakespeare's *Henry IV,* Part 2

country of the Psalmist ... fatness: 'Thou crownest the year with thy goodness; and thy paths drop fatness'. Psalm 65:11

wambling: *(dial)* walking unsteadily
turmit-head: *(dial)* turnip-head, simpleton
larry: *(dial)* disturbance

Chapter 29

After she has walked a mile along the road to Port-Bredy, Lucetta returns towards Casterbridge. On her way back she meets Elizabeth. At this very moment they see a bull with a staff attached to a ring in its nose coming towards them; they flee into a nearby barn into which the bull pursues them and contrives to shut the door accidentally. It chases them back and forth until they are happily rescued from their predicament by Henchard. Lucetta is hysterically grateful for her rescue, but as Henchard leads her homeward she confesses that during her absence from home she has married Farfrae. Approaching Casterbridge they hear the bells ringing and the town band playing to celebrate the wedding.

Not only Henchard's physical strength, but also his courage is evident in this encounter with the bull. Yet at the moment when happiness seems to be once more within his grasp it is snatched from him again by the news of Lucetta's marriage.

NOTES AND GLOSSARY:

Yahoo: The Yahoos in Book 4 of Swift's *Gulliver's Travels* (1726) are degenerate brutes with some apparent affinities to the human race

Abrahamic success: a reference to the prolific descendants of Abraham; see, for instance, Genesis 13:16, 'I will make thy seed as the dust of the earth: so that if a man can number the dust of the earth, then shall thy seed also be numbered'

Gurth's . . . brass: Gurth is a swineherd in Sir Walter Scott's *Ivanhoe* (1820); he is a serf and wears a brass collar welded round his neck, with his owner's name engraved on it

Chapter 30

Lucetta confesses to Farfrae that she has not yet told Elizabeth of their marriage and she goes upstairs to do so. Though distressed at the depth of Elizabeth's disapproval, she begs her to stay on with them in High-Place Hall. After Lucetta leaves her, however, Elizabeth decides to go away and she immediately arranges a lodging for herself not far from Henchard's house.

Interest here focuses on Elizabeth who expresses the view of Lucetta's marriage which would be the one generally accepted at the time by people who knew the true circumstances. However, Elizabeth is in possession of facts unknown to most of the townsfolk.

NOTES AND GLOSSARY:

John Gilpin: from William Cowper's ballad of that name (1782). Gilpin too delayed a journey in order to attend to customers

Video . . . sequor: from *Metamorphoses,* VII:21, 'I see and approve of better things, but I follow after the worse.' The *Metamorphoses* is a Latin poem by Ovid (43BC–AD17) which recounts mythical transformation

Nathan tones: accusingly; 'And Nathan said to David, Thou art the man'. 2 Samuel 12:1–14

Chapter 31

Henchard's unfortunate business transactions, together with the revelation made by the furmity-woman, result in a complete reversal of his fortunes and he becomes bankrupt. The complete integrity of his character is revealed by his extremely honest dealings with his creditors. He now leaves his house and goes to lodge with Jopp, but when Elizabeth tries to visit him he will not see her. She later learns that Farfrae has bought up Henchard's business.

The positions of Henchard and Farfrae are now completely reversed, but this reversal is accompanied by a swing in the reader's sympathy from Farfrae to Henchard. In adversity Henchard shows himself to be fair and honest; on the other hand, Farfrae, now a very rich man, is governed only by his business acumen: when he buys up Henchard's business he makes the men work harder and pays them less.

Chapter 32

At the lower end of Casterbridge stand two bridges, one of brick and one of stone. Here those down on their luck go to think on their misfortunes, and here Michael Henchard goes in his troubles. One afternoon while he is there Jopp passes by and tells him that Farfrae has moved into his old house. A little later Farfrae himself stops beside Henchard and tries to persuade him to come and live in part of his old house, but Henchard cannot accept this generous offer. A reconciliation is brought about between Elizabeth and her step-father when she looks after him in an illness; this gives him hope for the future again and he takes a job with Farfrae as a journeyman hay-trusser. Whilst he is working in this way the twenty-one years of his vow of abstinence come to an end.

In this chapter Henchard is shown in relationship to Jopp, to Farfrae and to Elizabeth, and through the latter the possibility of his redemption is seen; yet this grain of hope is swiftly followed by the news that he has started drinking again. This recalls the opening chapter of the novel and the disastrous consequences of Henchard's intemperance.

NOTES AND GLOSSARY:

Prophet's chamber: a small room like that prepared for the prophet Elisha; 'Let us make a little chamber . . . on the wall; and let us set for him here a bed, and a table, and a stool, and a candlestick . . .' 2 Kings 4:10

wise in her generation: 'The children of this world are in their generation wiser than the children of light.' St Luke 16:8

Chapter 33

Henchard decides to end his years of abstinence at the Three Mariners. There he awaits the church choir and insists on their singing for him some particularly harsh and threatening verses from the 109th Psalm; he then tells them that they have been singing of Farfrae. One day whilst at work he has a bitter encounter with Lucetta and later, after an incident in the loft of the corn-store, Elizabeth feels that she must warn Farfrae against Henchard.

Though the worst side of Henchard now predominates, he is not unscrupulous enough to ruin Lucetta by making use of her foolish note to him. Yet his increasing bitterness towards Farfrae arouses a feeling of suspense in the reader.

NOTES AND GLOSSARY:

ballets: a kind of madrigal
rantipole: *(dial)* wild
'Mistress . . . man's love': But, mistress, know yourself; down on your knees,/ And thank heaven, fasting, for a good man's love (Shakespeare, *As You Like It*, III. v. 57-8)

Chapter 34

Next day Elizabeth tells Farfrae to beware of Henchard and this warning, together with comments made by other folk in the town, causes him to abandon a project he had of establishing Henchard in a little seed-shop. Lucetta fears disclosure and tries to persuade Farfrae to leave Casterbridge, but at this moment he is invited to become Mayor and he determines to stay. Lucetta again asks Henchard to return her letters, hoping to destroy his hold over her. However, Henchard remembers that they are in his old safe in the house where Lucetta and Farfrae now live. He goes to collect them, planning to disclose the whole story to Farfrae, but though he reads some of the letters aloud to Farfrae he cannot bring himself to betray Lucetta.

Lucetta's rash foolishness is again apparent here and once more attention is focused on her letters. Farfrae's ambition is seen to work against his hope of personal happiness when he agrees to become Mayor, whilst Henchard is shown to be a better character than he himself believes.

NOTES AND GLOSSARY:

Tamerlane's trumpet: the army of the great eastern conqueror Tamerlane (Timur the Lame, 1330–1405) was said to use trumpets seven feet long
Aphrodite: Greek goddess of love

Chapter 35

It chances that Lucetta overhears part of the scene being played between Henchard and Farfrae and although her secret has been kept she is terrified. Next day she writes to Henchard begging him to meet her at the Ring that afternoon. The sentimental memory of his meeting there with Susan, together with Lucetta's drawn looks, persuade him to stop persecuting Lucetta and he promises to send her the letters next day.

Lucetta's anguish has been brought about by her failure to disclose the mistakes of her past to Farfrae before their marriage; this is a tragic device which Hardy uses several times in his novels. Lucetta's rashness is again emphasised, first by her writing to Henchard, and secondly by her arranging to meet him secretly.

Chapter 36

As she returns home Lucetta is approached by Jopp who asks her to intercede with Farfrae to get him a position; she refuses and dismisses him. Later Henchard asks Jopp to deliver the parcel of letters to Lucetta. On the way to Lucetta's house Jopp visits the inn called Peter's Finger and there he undoes the parcel and reads the letters aloud. The ill-assorted company at the inn decides to arrange a skimmity-ride to punish Lucetta for her loose behaviour. The package is then resealed and returned to Lucetta next morning. Whilst discussion of the skimmity-ride is going on, however, a stranger visits Peter's Finger and then proceeds towards Casterbridge.

Here Hardy introduces a somewhat sinister note, with his description of Mixen Lane and Peter's Finger; Jopp who has already appeared as a threatening figure now fulfils his function of villainy. Suspense is created by the arrival of the stranger.

NOTES AND GLOSSARY:

Adullam: a refuge; 'David ... escaped to the cave Adullam ... And every one that was in distress, and every one that was in debt, and every one that was discontented, gathered themselves unto him.' 1 Samuel 22:1–2

Ashton ... Ravenswood: in Sir Walter Scott's novel, *The Bride of Lammermoor* (1819), Chapter 35, Colonel Ashton was waiting to fight a duel with the Lord of Ravenswood; Ravenswood rode towards him and then suddenly disappeared; he had been sucked down by quicksands

swingels: cudgels

oven-pyle: long-handled wooden shovel for putting loaves into oven

Chapter 37

A brief royal visit to Casterbridge provides the occasion for local celebrations. A loyal address is prepared which Farfrae, as Mayor, is to read. Henchard asks to join the Council in their homage but they refuse his request; however, when the day comes, dressed in his old clothes he steps forward with a home-made flag to offer his own welcome. Farfrae roughly orders him away and Henchard goes, but the local ladies cause Lucetta some distress when they talk of him as Farfrae's old patron. After the official welcome the crowds drift away. Plans have been completed to hold the skimmity-ride that very night.

Henchard is now almost at the depths of his degradation; at the same time Hardy shows Farfrae already past his zenith; the authoritative mayor is less popular than the penniless young man was and Lucetta feels that she is being snubbed by the local people.

NOTES AND GLOSSARY:

fête carillonnée:	*(French)* festival marked by a special peal of bells
Calphurnia:	Caesar's wife in Shakespeare (1564–1616)'s play, *Julius Caesar*
Pharaoh's chariots:	when Moses and the Israelites were being pursued by the Egyptians, God 'took off their [the Egyptians] chariot wheels, that they drave them heavily'. Exodus 14:25
hontish:	*(dial)* proud
toppered:	toppled down

Chapter 38

Henchard is now anxious for revenge and he asks Farfrae to meet him in the corn loft. He awaits him with one arm tightly bound and tells the younger man that they are to fight until one of them is thrown out of the upper door which has a forty-foot drop below. After a fierce struggle Henchard gains the upper hand, but he cannot bring himself to kill his old friend. Farfrae is released and leaves. Henchard, horrified at his own action, is numb; in this state he hears Farfrae say that he is going to Weatherbury and decides to await his return and beg his forgiveness.

Henchard's impetuosity leads him into yet another rash action, yet an action oddly governed by the rules of fair play; the paradoxes of violence and gentlemanliness, hate and affection are deeply ingrained in Henchard's character.

NOTES AND GLOSSARY:

Weltlust:	*(German)* worldly pleasure

Chapter 39

After his encounter with Henchard, Farfrae prepares to drive to Budmouth but a note arrives asking him to go to Weatherbury so he changes his plans. The note is a clumsy contrivance to remove him from home while the skimmity-ride takes place. Waiting for his return Lucetta listens to the distant noise of the skimmity-ride and the more immediate conversation of two maid-servants speaking from upper windows. She hears herself and Henchard described as the figures caricatured in the skimmity-ride. Just at that moment Elizabeth enters and tries to close the shutters, but Lucetta, now hysterical, insists on looking out and when she sees the effigy of herself in the procession she falls in a fit. The doctor is sent for and orders Farfrae's man to fetch him from Budmouth. Meanwhile the actors in the skimmity-ride seem to have disappeared without trace.

Hardy's delight in old country customs is seen here in his description of the skimmity-ride and of the cunning manoeuvres of its perpetrators.

NOTES AND GLOSSARY:

felo de se: *(Latin)* suicide (he means murder)

the crew of Comus: in the masque of this name by John Milton (1608–74), Comus, the god of riotous mirth, was accompanied by a group of noisy revellers who would disappear at his bidding

---

Chapter 40

After seeing the skimmity-ride Henchard feels restless. He goes to visit Elizabeth and follows her to Farfrae's house where he learns of Lucetta's illness. He goes to meet Farfrae to persuade him to return home, but the younger man will not believe his message and goes on to Mellstock. When Farfrae finally returns home he is able to comfort his wife briefly before she dies. Meanwhile Henchard returns home and Jopp tells him that a sea-captain has been looking for him.

The pathos surrounding Lucetta's death helps towards a reconciliation between Henchard and Elizabeth. Yet anticipation and some foreboding is aroused by the arrival of the sea-captain.

NOTES AND GLOSSARY:

repentant . . . joy in heaven: '. . . joy shall be in heaven over one sinner that repenteth' St Luke 15:7

Chapter 41

After her vigil with Lucetta, Elizabeth visits Henchard who, seeing she is tired, persuades her to rest in another room whilst he prepares breakfast. While she sleeps, Newson, her real father, arrives but when Henchard tells him that Elizabeth is dead he goes away and leaves Casterbridge immediately. Henchard, now overwhelmed with affection for Elizabeth, fears that Newson will return and decides to throw himself into the weirpool. He makes his way there only to see his own effigy floating on the water. He takes this as a sign and returns home again where his reconciliation with Elizabeth is completed and she offers to go and live with him again.

The dramatic turn of events in this chapter is a typical Hardyesque view of the irony of fate, for at the moment when Henchard thinks he has regained Elizabeth's love her real father returns. Suspense is maintained, however, when Newson proves not to have lost his youthful naïvety.

Chapter 42

Newson does not return, and Henchard settles with Elizabeth in a small seed-shop bought for him by the Town Council. A year passes and his trade develops but he is distressed to discover that there is a growing attachment between Elizabeth and Farfrae.

At this point of the novel the plot remains fairly static. Hardy sets about rehabilitating Henchard and shows us Farfrae much chastened, and less proud of his high position.

NOTES AND GLOSSARY:

Time, 'in his own grey style': 'Young Love should teach Time, in his own grey style'; see 'Epipsychidion', 55, by Percy Bysshe Shelley (1792–1822)

plumes . . . Juno's bird . . . Argus eyes: Argus in Greek mythology, had a hundred eyes and only two slept at one time, but Mercury lulled him to sleep with his lyre and killed him; Juno then put his eyes in her peacock's tail

solicitus timor: *(Latin)* anxious fear

Chapter 43

Henchard considers what he will do when the wedding between Elizabeth and Farfrae takes place; he decides that he will accept anything to be near her. Then one day he sees Newson approaching the town and he decides to go away. He leaves the town dressed in much the same way as when he had entered it many years before. When he has gone Farfrae takes Elizabeth to his house and there she is reunited with her true father, Richard Newson, who tells them how Henchard deceived him. This turns Elizabeth against Henchard.

The wheel has now turned full circle and Henchard is seen again as he was at the opening of the story, but now he is alone without wife or child. His sense of loneliness and alienation is deeply moving and is highlighted by the contrasting geniality and sociability of Newson.

NOTES AND GLOSSARY:

I—Cain—go alone . . . I can bear: 'And Cain said unto the Lord, My punishment is greater than I can bear. Behold, thou hast driven me out this day from the face of the earth.' Genesis 4:13–14

Chapter 44

Henchard first visits Weydon-Priors to retrace his steps that fateful day so many years ago. Then he takes work as a hay-trusser, just as he did at that time, but now the spirit has gone out of him. When he meets a carrier who has lately come from Casterbridge he learns that Elizabeth's wedding-day is approaching so he decides to go and try to make his peace with her. He buys himself new clothes and a caged goldfinch as a present for her. He arrives at Farfrae's house in the evening of the wedding-day but Elizabeth rebuffs him and he leaves, vowing never to bother her again. In going he forgets the goldfinch which he had placed under a hedge.

A sense of impending tragedy now pervades the book. The futility of Henchard's struggle against Fate is made apparent by his return to the very state he was in when the story began and is underlined by his lack of hope. His isolation is emphasised by the contrast between him and the joyful participants in the wedding celebrations.

NOTES AND GLOSSARY:

out-Farfraed Farfrae: was more like Farfrae than Farfrae himself; the term is taken from Shakespeare's 'out-herods Herod' in *Hamlet*, III. 2. 17

'the shade . . . upthrown': Henchard is moved by the thought that he had tried to take Newson's daughter from him; the quotation is from Shelley's *The Revolt of Islam*, VIII. 6. 2

Chapter 45

Soon after her wedding Elizabeth finds the goldfinch dead under a hedge, but it is not until several weeks later that she learns that Henchard had brought it with him. This discovery sends her and Farfrae out to find him. After a long search they see Abel Whittle who tells them that Henchard has just died. His bitter will, aimed at wiping out all memory of himself, is pinned to the head of his bed. Elizabeth is greatly moved by Henchard's death and regrets her unkindness to him.

This is an intensely moving ending, for not only is the good-natured Elizabeth left to live with an action that she must always regret, but also the genuine kind-heartedness of Henchard is made apparent through Abel Whittle's words. The final reflections of the book, though they are Elizabeth's, are typical of Hardy's gloomy thoughts about life.

NOTES AND GLOSSARY:

'whose gestures . . . mind': Elizabeth's growing understanding of life was reflected in her face; the quotation is from Shelley's *The Revolt of Islam*, I. 54. 5

Diana Multimammia: the 'many-breasted Diana'; Diana was the Roman fertility goddess

Capharnaum: Capernaum; Jesus went to dwell in Capernaum and thus fulfilled the words of the prophet Esaias, 'The people which sat in darkness saw great light; and to them which sat in the region and shadow of death light is sprung up'. See St Matthew 4:13–16

Part 3

Commentary

General comment

The novel as tragedy

Though the book opens with three travellers on a lonely road leading to a country village, *The Mayor of Casterbridge*, unlike Hardy's earlier novels, is concerned with urban rather than rural life. Its principal setting is the town of Casterbridge, the capital of Hardy's Wessex, and its principal actors are men engaged in commerce. Yet Casterbridge is intimately bound up with the surrounding countryside; the business of the town is concerned with buying and selling farm animals and produce; the bustle of the weekly market is the centre of the town's life; the local labourers work in the hay-yards and the cattle markets; the shops sell tools and implements for agricultural and pastoral life. 'Casterbridge was,' Hardy comments, 'in most respects but the pole, focus or nerve-knot of the surrounding country life.' (Chapter 9)

The town reflects, however, not only the working life of the agricultural community in its environs, but it also gives weight to a class system which touches, but scarcely troubles, the lives of the country folk around; in Casterbridge it is seen to be a hierarchy, reflected in broader outlines and in larger numbers, the influence of which is omnipresent. It is exemplified by the customers of the three inns of the town; the King's Arms, the chief hotel, where George III had once stopped to change horses, is patronised by 'the gentle-people and such like leading volk' (Chapter 5); it is where Michael Henchard is seen in his prosperity, chairing a great public dinner; the Three Mariners is the inn attended by 'a secondary set of worthies' (Chapter 6); it is where Michael Henchard, down on his luck, no longer Mayor and with his fortunes in rapid decline, chooses to end his vow of abstinence; Peter's Finger is the home of the dregs of Casterbridge society; it is the place where the scheme for the skimmity-ride is hatched, a mockery devised simultaneously to deride Henchard and to parody the ceremony of the royal visit. Likewise, the two bridges where the unfortunate of the town sigh their time away show a 'marked difference of quality' (Chapter 32). In Casterbridge a man can rise, and can be seen to rise, in prosperity and fame; there too, of course, a man's fall and his ensuing misery are on display. It is an ideal setting for a tragedy of ambition.

Yet the town itself plays a more vital role in the novel than as a mere setting. A sense of history, closely juxtaposed with the sense of place, pervades the book and suggests both change and continuity. History is seen to have happened in the passing of the Romans; history is seen happening in Michael Henchard's abandonment of the country for the town, in his rise from poverty to wealth and civic success, and in his final ousting by a rival from even further afield. Thus his story is universalised and becomes at one and the same time an individual tragedy and part of the experience of man.

The novel charts a period of expansion for Casterbridge itself, but a period of destruction of the old ways of Wessex life: Weydon-Priors Fair deteriorates, the mechanical improvements of the age serving merely to emphasise its frivolous side; country people not adaptable to change, such as the furmity-woman, lose their livelihood, whilst others have to learn new skills or, like Henchard, abandon their country pursuits and move to the town, exploiting their knowledge of agricultural life in a new business situation. The town with its much larger community offers scope for advancement of which the scattered life of the agricultural Wessex countryside knows nothing. The ambitions of Michael Henchard are likely to come to nothing whilst he remains a hay-trusser; in the country, power and status are out of his reach, but in Casterbridge his dream of being worth a thousand pounds becomes a possibility and ultimately a reality.

The passing of the old settled country life is emphasised by the fact that all three of the principal male characters – Henchard, Farfrae and Newson – are migrants to Casterbridge. Newson, the sailor, is, of course, a natural wanderer, and throughout the book settles nowhere for long. Michael Henchard, however, is a genuine countryman, a Wessex labourer; he is itinerant when the novel begins, but his encounter with the turnip-hoer suggests that his skilled country craft is little in demand; with the disappearance of his wife and daughter Henchard, young, strong and ambitious, makes for Casterbridge where he settles to a new life, buying and selling corn and hay, turning into a business the agricultural commodities upon which his country skills had depended. The reader does not follow his rise in the world, but the pattern of it was, no doubt, that of the archetypal new middle-class man of the first half of the nineteenth century. The Corn Laws of 1815 kept the price of corn artificially high; not only the farmers, but those who dealt in corn were able to increase their wealth swiftly; thus Henchard, starting with nothing but his will to work and his ambition, rapidly expands his business, buys a grand house close to his factor's yard and eventually becomes Mayor of Casterbridge.

This could have been the end of a success story, but Hardy turns it into the beginning of a tragedy. He was not interested in his protagonist's upward struggle, but rather in the events which conspired together finally to defeat him. Is it possible to point to any one happening and say,'*That* is where Henchard's tragedy began'? Hardy himself does just this in Chapter 6 when he introduces Farfrae to us, for Farfrae happens to pass the King's Arms at the very moment when the bad bread is being discussed. Had he passed on as he intended, Hardy comments, 'this history had never been enacted'. As it is, he stops for a moment to assist Henchard by a generous deed and remains to assist in his ruin. When the young Scotsman arrives in Casterbridge he is as Michael Henchard was nineteen years before; he has little but his ambition to help him on his way and he intends to start a new life. In fact, we never learn anything of his life before his advent in Casterbridge. He is, as Henchard was to a lesser extent, an intruder from outside; we do not know whom, if anyone, Henchard displaced, but in the displacing of Henchard himself Hardy retells the old old story of the struggle between the generations. With knowledge and new skills to back up his ambitions, Farfrae is to Henchard the threat of youth to age; it is inevitable that his efficiency should displace the more rough and ready methods of his elder. Ironically, Henchard himself is the first to recognise this and to voice his realisation of it to the younger man. 'In my business, 'tis true that strength and bustle build up a firm,' he tells Farfrae, 'But judgment and knowledge are what keep it established' (Chapter 7). Implicit in his words is a belief in the peaceful co-existence of both modes of life. Hardy's understanding is the more painful one, that new ideas, new methods must displace the old and it is this tension between adherence to the established ways of life, the simple pursuits of country crafts and skills, and the progressive, not to say revolutionary, movements of the nineteenth century, the economic manipulation of agriculture and the industrialisation of farming, that Hardy explores in this novel.

Douglas Brown suggests that the seasonal cycle of *The Mayor of Casterbridge* relates the theme of the book to the ancient seasonal myth in which renewal can take place only after the death of the current priest or king. The novel can certainly bear this general interpretation and Hardy, by giving it a historical perspective, emphasises again the universality of the theme that, since time began, the prerequisite for change, for progress, has been the displacement of what already exists in order to make way for new ideas. Though such changes occur slowly, they occur relentlessly; thus, Roman Casterbridge is little more than a historic memory whilst the character of the Casterbridge of the Corn Law is seen to be altering as the story takes place. The main interest of the plot is in the rise and fall of Michael Henchard and in the closely related rise of Donald Farfrae; the love theme hinging on the confused and fickle love of Lucetta and the steady fidelity of Elizabeth-Jane is completely subordinated to the larger notion of the old order changing and yielding place to the new. However, once this general framework for the novel has been set up, Hardy's main concern with it is to exploit through the character of Michael Henchard the potential for tragedy which it possesses, for the novel is, as he insists in his Preface, a 'study of one man's deeds and character.' This complicated interplay between setting, mythology, plot and character is what gives the novel its power and fascination.

Certainly *The Mayor of Casterbridge* is a novel which can be read again and again; Hardy was nothing if not a good story-teller. 'A story must be exceptional enough to justify its telling,' he asserted, and serial publication encouraged him to ensure that there were enough exceptional incidents to entertain any reader. Narrative devices abound: Henchard and Lucetta are both characters with a hidden and disreputable secret in their past; the disappearance of Susan with the sailor early in the novel is counter-balanced by her reappearance in Chapter 3 and the more dramatic reappearance later of Newson himself; the letters of Lucetta and of Susan are used to give unexpected twists to the plot; dramatic or melodramatic incidents there are in plenty, from the sale of Susan, through the encounter with the mad bull and the desperate fight between Henchard and Farfrae to the skimmity-ride and the collapse and death of Lucetta; these and many more ensure a constant surface excitement in the novel. However, whilst Hardy believed that a novelist had to relate something more unusual than ordinary experiences, he knew that the success of a novel lay in adjusting the unusual to 'things eternal and universal'. Thus, it is his use of the narrative devices, not the devices themselves, that is significant. The first chapter is a good example.

The book does not open, as we are too frequently told, with the dramatic sale of a wife. It opens in a minor key, with solitary walkers on a lonely road. A mood of discordance is subtly introduced through the total lack of communication and the absence of any appearance of genuine human relationship between the man and the woman. Though the countryside may be, and probably is, beautiful, it is presented only as the travellers see it – a thick hoar of dust carpeting the road, the hedgerow and the edge of the stream likewise powdered by it; the vegetation is 'blackened-green'; the leaves are 'doomed'; a bird sings with 'weak' voice and his song is 'trite'. The sense of waste and decay is accentuated by the turnip-hoer's account of the destruction of Weydon-Priors village. Even the good, health-giving furmity is secretly corrupted and is one with the corruption of the mis-spelt English language by which it is advertised. The bizarre sale of Susan and Elizabeth-Jane is now seen as a culmination of the decay and corruption around; the resulting loss in human dignity for seller and sold prepares the reader for the tragedy which seems inevitable from such an opening. Nor is it only repercussions from the wife-sale that reverberate through the book; the picture of the lonely figures on a deserted road is a recurrent image and serves as a patterning feature too, bringing the wheel full circle when Henchard at the end sets out on the road away from Casterbridge, older and wearier, with less spring in his stride and with his shoulders weighted down by his state of hopelessness as well as by his hay-trusser's basket.

Another example, different in kind, is Susan Henchard's last letter to her husband. Manifestly a story-teller's device, with the mystery of the inscription on the envelope, the dying woman's struggle to write it and her shattering revelation which comes to Michael as if from the grave, it is used to illuminate plot, form and character at the same time. The ironic twist it gives to the plot holds within it another, hidden, irony, for had Henchard obeyed his wife's request the agony of his knowledge would have been delayed and it is his knowledge of the truth of Elizabeth's paternity, not the fact itself, which eats into him like a canker. Yet only such a character as Susan, weak-willed, fearful of her husband, even more fearful of the eternal guilt of wrongdoing, could write a letter of such portent and seal it so incompetently; only a Michael Henchard who had always ridden roughshod over his wife's desires could so easily dismiss her dying wish and in doing so bring upon himself Fate's revenge for Susan's wasted years.

Despite the multiplicity of incident and coincidence, the story is in the main convincing. Though to modern readers the sale of a wife may seem incredible, Hardy tells us in his Preface that it was based upon an actual event which occurred about the time to which the novel alludes, and he himself found accounts of no fewer than three such sales which had occured in Wessex in the mid-1820s. If any thread in the story is weaker than the rest, it is perhaps the introduction of a second disreputable secret in Henchard's past, his liaison in Jersey with Lucetta. Such an involvement is necessary to the story in order for the many-sided antagonism between Henchard and Farfrae to develop, but it remains slightly unconvincing, as too does the later misjudgement of Farfrae in regard to Lucetta and Elizabeth-Jane. However, what appears to be a slight flaw in an otherwise admirably constructed and skilfully executed plot is easily overlooked in the actual reading of the novel.

Description and language

Stylistically, what makes the greatest impact is the book's visual quality. Attention has already been drawn (above) to the lonely figures seen wandering in empty landscapes and Professor Norman Page comments on one of Hardy's favourite descriptive devices in this novel, the 'framing' of a scene by showing it as an observer may see it through a window. After her return Susan first observes her husband in this way through a window at the King's Arms where he is presiding at a big dinner; later the market and its figures are several times observed from the vantage point of an upper room in High-Place Hall and near the end of the book Henchard watches Elizabeth's wedding festivities through an open doorway. It is not only the 'framed' pictures, however, but the sheer visual quality of all the description which impresses – the details of the church tower in Chapter 4, the old Casterbridge houses and their gardens in Chapter 9, the contrasting fêtes arranged by Henchard and Farfrae in Chapter 16.

Above all, however, descriptions of clothes abound. In the nineteenth century clothes were worn rather like a 'class uniform'. The labourer could be seen to be a labourer by his mode of dress; the skilled craftsman would dress differently again, even to the distinguishing marks of his particular craft. Higher up the scale dress would be formal and immediately recognisable as the mark of a certain status. The second paragraph of the novel immediately identifies Michael Henchard at that stage of his career; with his brown corduroy jacket, fustian waistcoat and breeches, tanned leggings and a straw hat, he is no common labourer, but a skilled hay-trusser; even the white horn buttons on his waistcoat are a symbol of his superiority. When we first see him after the lapse of time during which he has become Mayor, he is 'dressed in an old-fashioned evening suit, an expanse of frilled shirt showing on his broad breast; jewelled studs and a heavy gold chain'. Hardy draws attention to these two contrasting modes of dress a number of times throughout the novel, for they chart the social rise and fall of Michael Henchard. Men and women rarely dressed at odds with their social position; those who did were generally on the downward path; so Henchard's sense of failure, of degradation, is apparent in the way he clings after his bankruptcy and fall from power to the shabby gentility of clothes unsuited to his labours, the 'old blue cloth suit of his gentlemanly times, a rusty silk hat, and a once black satin stock, soiled and shabby.' His loss of human dignity is emphasised by the juxtaposed description, with its gay epithets, of the way he dressed in his youth in 'clean, suitable clothes, light and cheerful in hue; leggings yellow as marigolds, corduroys immaculate as new flax, and a neckerchief like a flower-garden' (Chapter 32).

Elizabeth-Jane, too, is codified by her manner of dress. When she arrives in Casterbridge, still in mourning for Newson, she is dressed simply in an old-fashioned black suit; as the mayor's step-daughter she buys a black silk bonnet, a velvet mantle and a sunshade and is transformed. Later, when her circumstances change and she leaves High-Place Hall after Lucetta's marriage to Farfrae, she takes off 'her pretty dress and arrays herself in a plain one.' The function of clothes in defining and giving personality to the wearer is explained by Lucetta when she is called upon to decide between a cherry-coloured gown and a lighter one for the coming season: 'settling upon new clothes is so trying... You are that person... or you are *that* totally different person... for the whole of the coming spring: and one of the two, you don't know which, may turn out to be very objectionable' (Chapter 24).

Whilst clothes have a useful function in the novel in helping to define characters and background they also serve as a part of the patterned framework of the book, giving it unity and compactness, referring the reader backwards and forwards in order to understand the intricate social movement of the various characters.

The strong pictorial element of the novel is reflected in the language with its rich allusive content. By far the major source of allusion is the Bible and related sources. In Victorian England, and particularly in rural and small urban communities, the Church was the centre of life. Hardy himself had many connections with the local church where his father and grandfather had played in the orchestra. In *The Life* he tells how, as a boy, he attended church regularly twice every Sunday, 'till he knew the Morning and Evening Services by heart... as well as large portions of the New Version of the Psalms'. Church services, hymns, the Bible were fully absorbed into his mental background and formed an almost subconscious part of his intellectual equipment, though in later life he became sceptical of religious teaching. In an earlier novel, *Under the Greenwood Tree,* Hardy had used a disagreement within the hierarchy of the village church as one of the main plot threads. It is the only novel where the Church plays quite such a central role, but in a number of the novels significant aspects of the Church or church life are introduced, and in all of them his readers' acquaintance with Church and Bible is taken for granted. The language of *The Mayor of Casterbridge* is enriched by many biblical references and similes, such as the description of Elizabeth-Jane's first visit to Henchard when Jopp slips in before her, 'like the quicker cripple at Bethesda'. In Chapter 24 when the seed-drill is brought into the market-place Hardy even implies adverse criticism of Lucetta for being unable to take part in the exchange between Elizabeth and Farfrae based on various biblical texts concerned with sowing.

Whilst such allusions may briefly illuminate particular moments in the book, others have more far-reaching importance in the texture of the whole novel. An excellent example of this is when Henchard realises that Newson has returned and will supersede him in Elizabeth's affection. As he leaves Casterbridge he proclaims, 'I – Cain – go alone as I deserve – an outcast and a vagabond. But my punishment is *not* greater than I can bear' and all the wealth of the biblical story is here evoked to enrich the reader's view of Henchard's tragic history; his sense of alienation from God and man, his isolation and his tremendous fortitude in the face of adversity are all brought out, first in his comparison of himself with Cain, but secondly in his defiant contrast with the biblical figure, his rejection of Cain's capitulation to God's punishment. The reader less well acquainted with the Bible than Hardy is unlikely to have difficulties with straightforward comprehension of the novel; the subtler layers of meaning brought into the story by such use of language are perhaps more difficult to come by.

Other major sources of allusion are the classics, folksong and various British authors from Shakespeare to Tennyson.

Allusions, similes and metaphors taken from literature and scripture are, however, not the only linguistic problem the reader has to face. Interwoven with these is the language which belongs to the life of Wessex in the nineteenth century. It is not merely the homespun vocabulary, the dialect words and the malapropisms which give us pause, but many of the words which Hardy uses naturally as part of his everyday language – the 'dimity curtains' of the High Street houses, the 'mattocks', 'butter-firkins' and 'seed-lips' on sale in the shops, the brown 'holland' overcoat which Henchard slips over his dress-suit after the public dinner at the King's Arms, or the 'fly' which Elizabeth-Jane takes from Henchard's house to High-Place Hall. These words and many more have dropped out of common usage and create at least some difficulty on a first reading, though the meaning of many of them subsequently becomes self-evident. Through his language, as much as through his treatment of the socio-historical background, Hardy achieves the flavour and atmosphere of a Wessex life now past and which is preserved in the pages of his novels. To savour the full enjoyment of what he offers it is perhaps necessary to understand the meaning and significance of every word he writes; nevertheless, judicious use of a good dictionary and of annotations can enable every reader to go some way along the path towards this perfectionist policy.

Characters

Michael Henchard

It has been suggested above (p. 43) that Hardy's main concern in this novel is with the character of Michael Henchard. The full title of the book is *The Life and Death of the Mayor of Casterbridge* and it is subtitled *A Story of a Man of Character*. Who then is this 'man of character' upon whom there is so much concentration on the title-page? Why does Hardy present him as a tragic hero?

He is seen first as an anonymous character, a figure in a landscape of which he appears to be part, dust lying indifferently on the road he travels, on his shoes, on his clothes. An observer's eye describes him, picking out the salient features of his person and of his dress, differentiating him from other such travellers only in a general way, showing him as a skilled countryman, as a hay-trusser, as a husband and father. A sense of resignation hangs about him, however; though he is a hay-trusser and it is the hay-trussing season, there appears to be little prospect of his finding a job and even less of his being able to house himself and his family. Even at this stage he seems destined for the blows rather than for the blessings of life. He appears as an isolated and alienated figure; though walking together with his wife and child there is no communion between them and by looking neither to right nor to left, not attending to the woman beside him, but keeping his eyes fixed on a ballad sheet before his face, he is locked in the world of his own thoughts, silent and lonely.

The spell is broken as they approach the village of Weydon-Priors when the noises of the fair impinge upon the silence and the coming of the turnip-hoer introduces a sense of community, but the image of the isolated mythic figure persists throughout the book.

At the fair, Henchard, though still unnamed, is gradually individualised by his words and actions. He begins by giving way to his wife's urgent request to go with her and the child into the furmity tent, rather than into that where beer, ale and cider are being sold. This is the only selfless action he performs, for he swiftly discovers that furmity laced with illicit rum is more to his palate than in its simple state and he is soon the worse for drink. He becomes a different character, talking loudly in contrast to his earlier taciturnity, and making himself one with the company in the furmity tent. Now the worse side of his nature gains control. He becomes quarrelsome and rails against his lot in life. 'If I were a free man again,' he meditates aloud, and this thought is followed by the impetuous sale of his wife, by which he makes himself free to follow his ambitions.

Certainly both Henchard and Farfrae are ambitious men and many critics have claimed that the novel is about ambition. Merryn Williams, for instance, maintains, 'Henchard wants to get rid of his wife and child because he thinks they are preventing him from making a fortune'. To what extent is this a true statement of fact? It *is* what Henchard implies in the furmity tent, but we should remind ourselves that he was drunk at the time. As he himself comments of Susan in Chapter 2, 'She knows I am not in my senses when I do that'. Ian Gregor is more to the mark when he talks of 'ambivalences' in the novel, for though Henchard would perhaps like to be free again and though he believes his wife and child are preventing him from getting on in the world, nevertheless when he is sober he has no thought of allowing Susan and the child to go and declares, 'Well, I must walk about till I find her'. Chapter 2 is, in fact, a reversal of the narration in Chapter 1. Henchard, now cold sober, regrets his rash act, renounces the strong drink for which he had craved the previous night, and endeavours to get Susan back. He is no longer an anonymous figure, for we learn his name for the first time during his vow in the church. Contrary to the idea that he is ruled by ambition, he spends many months and every penny he has, even to the sailor's five guineas, in a fruitless effort to get Susan back. At last, believing his search to be hopeless, he traverses the road towards Casterbridge in much the same way as he entered the book, except that now he is alone in a physical sense as well. Thus, at the end of the two chapters which are essentially a prologue to the main story, we are left to wonder whether the bad or the good in Michael Henchard will triumph, whether the rash impetuosity, the drunkenness, the anger against life will overcome his better side, his regret, his desire to make amends, his intention to remain sober.

Nineteen years pass before we again see Michael Henchard. During this time he has prospered materially and more than fulfilled his own hopes, when he sat, jobless and almost penniless, in the furmity tent at Weydon-Priors. He has gained wealth and position, he has kept his vow and no longer drinks. Yet beneath the surface smoulders the same passion, the same impetuousness, though now kept under control by an iron will. Above all, he is still a lonely, isolated man and success has intensified his isolation. Because of his position as Mayor, as wealthy corn-factor, as employer of labour, he is vulnerable and it is his vulnerability which makes it impossible for him to attach himself in any personal way to others. The thoughtless sale enacted at Weydon-Priors, now a guilty secret and cause of shame in his past, leaves him married and not married. Jean Brooks suggests that in selling Susan he was substituting 'ambition for love', but as has been demonstrated above, the sale is not an act of conscious will, but an act committed in a state of inebriation, an act which, in his right mind, Michael Henchard regrets and would undo if he could. It is only subsequently that he is compelled to substitute ambition for love, since to allow love to grow between himself and any woman would serve to compound his crime against Susan. Hence, during the nineteen years following the sale of his wife Henchard has allowed his ambition to be his master and he has built himself up until he appears to stand on a pedestal and, with his ambitions fulfilled, a solitary man at the top, he has no further to go. His rehabilitation seems to be complete and represents years of struggle and self-control.

At this point in the story Henchard is a man who has allowed himself to become alienated both from his fellow men and from himself. But all his wealth and position cannot stop the gloomy moods of despair which sometimes descend upon him 'when the world seems to have the blackness of hell' (Chapter 12). The beginning of his downfall is the reversal of the substitution mentioned above. In his affair with Lucetta, despite the possible dire consequences of marriage with her, he substitutes love, or at least affection and gratitude, for ambition; in offering Farfrae a job he substitutes friendship for his own lonely power as supreme master of his corn and hay business.

Hardy constantly underlines the essentially fragile nature of Henchard's success by showing his repeated insufficiency in the face of adversity. Without Farfrae's knowledge he is unable to cure the 'grown' wheat and his failure to understand the principles of elementary economics is at least partly to blame for his bankruptcy. In addition to this, his lonely domestic life and desperate need for affection make him constantly dependent upon others for his own well-being; thus he gets entangled with Lucetta in Jersey and he sows the seeds of his own destruction by persuading Farfrae to stay in Casterbridge; when other human contacts fail he falls back on Jopp and finally clings to Elizabeth-Jane through a lie born of his heart's desolation, a lie simple and briefly effective, but one which leaves him no peace of mind to play out his remaining days.

On the credit side, not only has Henchard risen by his own endeavours and made every effort to atone for his earlier actions, but also he has deep-rooted ideas of justice and decency, too easily overlooked whilst we view the spectacle of his downfall. His behaviour at the time of his bankruptcy is exemplary, drawing from the Senior Commissioner the comment that he has 'never met a debtor who behaved more fairly' (Chapter 31); even in the terrible fight with Farfrae he refuses to take advantage of his superior strength and when he has Lucetta in his power he follows the only gentlemanly course open to him and returns her letters. The constant struggle between good and evil in him helps to raise him to tragic dimensions.

In adversity Henchard ceases to keep his passions under control. During the second half of the book there is a gradual reversion to the Henchard of Weydon-Priors fair. His vow comes to an end and he begins to drink again; his uncertain temper breaks out against his friend, Farfrae, against his workman, Abel Whittle, against his step-daughter, Elizabeth, against Lucetta, and it is frequently accompanied by physical or moral violence. By the time he leaves Casterbridge to become an itinerant hay-trusser again he has learned, however, through a series of humiliating and emotionally agonising incidents that love is more important than ambition and that a man can live without power and without wealth, provided that he has love. Thus, his desire to return to visit Elizabeth-Jane on her wedding day is prompted by his hope of salvaging her love from the wreck of his life:

> To make one attempt to be near her: to go back; to see her, to plead his cause before her, to ask forgiveness for his fraud, to endeavour strenuously to hold his own in her love; it was worth the risk of repulse, ay, of life itself. (Chapter 44)

It is, of course, too late. Like Shakespeare's Lear, with whom he has often been compared, he is destined to die bereft of the one who alone, despite his rough and unkind treatment of her, he realises he loves. The poignancy of his rejection by Elizabeth-Jane, which extinguishes his last feeble hope, is made more poignant by the contrasting fidelity of Abel Whittle whom Henchard in his prosperity had also treated harshly. Abel who had himself suffered at Henchard's hands had seen too the essential goodness beneath the stern exterior and he offers an epitaph to stand beside Henchard's own bleak and bitter one: 'He was kind-like to mother when she wer here below, sending her the best ship-coal . . . and taties, and such-like that were very needful to her'.

It is not possible to discuss Henchard merely in terms of his own character traits without looking also at the part played by the intervention of Fate in his life. In a number of Hardy's novels, but particularly in the later ones, Fate often appears to shape the plot, loading the dice against the protagonist. In *The Mayor of Casterbridge* a delicate balance is maintained between the ironies of Fate and the interaction of character; the principal form of Fate's intervention here is in the tragic conjunction of time, place, character and incident. The first of many such conjunctions occurs in Chapter 1 at Weydon-Priors Fair and is largely responsible, not for the sale taking place, but for its unfortunate outcome. When the auction begins the phlegmatic country folk, not surprisingly, make no bids at all. Only at the last moment, when the auction is about to collapse, does the sailor make his offer. Yet he is a casual visitor to the fair, whose brief entry into the furmity-tent happened to coincide with the final moments of the sale: 'He came in about five minutes ago,' says the furmity woman, 'And then 'a stepped back and then 'a looked in again'. Had he not entered the tent at the crucial moment the sale would have remained no more than a cruel humiliation to Susan and the whole story of Henchard's life would have been different.

Such ironies of time constantly recur throughout the novel, always closely associated with some aspect of character which gives irony its full play. Attention has already been drawn (p. 45) to the letter written by Susan to her husband revealing the truth about Elizabeth-Jane's paternity; another example can be found in the caprices of the harvest weather which drive Henchard to the verge of bankruptcy. The uncertainty of the harvest alone would have done little harm to a man with a flourishing business, conducting his buying and selling in a moderate fashion; combined, however, with Henchard's desire for revenge against Farfrae, his superstitious nature and his impetuosity it is a recipe for disaster. Again, the disclosure by the old furmity-woman at her appearance before the Petty Sessions in Casterbridge is riddled with ironic twists. She had all but forgotten the wife-sale in her tent so many years before had not first Michael himself and then Susan reminded her of it, Michael in his desire to trace his wife, and Susan in her effort to find him. Even the dramatic accusation at the court would have had less impact had Henchard's affairs been more stable and had he not the previous night wrung from the unwilling Lucetta an agreement to marry him. The dramatic irony of such incidents intensifies the tragic potential in Henchard's character and adds a fateful inevitability to the plot.

It is quite clear that Hardy intends the reader to sympathise with Henchard, despite all his faults. He towers above the other characters in the novel and the plot centres on his affairs in business and in love. The emotional impact of his downfall is extremely moving and Hardy, who is a master of pathos as well as of tragedy, tears at our heart-strings with little incidents such as that of the dead goldfinch as well as with the grandiose design ending in Henchard's tragic death. The minor characters are much less fully presented, but several need consideration.

Donald Farfrae

Donald Farfrae, like Henchard, is interesting not only as an individual, but also from the mythic point of view. As has been suggested above (p.43), he takes on Henchard's mantle in the new generation, displaces his old master and is himself crowned, a David to Henchard's Saul. There are also parallels with another biblical story, for Hardy shows Farfrae as a brother-figure, the Abel to Henchard's Cain, the one to whom the Lord speaks fair words whilst Henchard is rejected.

When we first meet Farfrae he is depicted as a pleasant engaging young man. Like the biblical David he is 'ruddy and of a fair countenance', but interestingly, considering Hardy's concentration on clothes in this novel, we are not told what he is wearing; yet he is clearly seen to be a stranger and some sense of his social position is accorded us from the fact that he carries a carpet-bag of 'smart floral pattern' and obviously fashionable. Like Henchard he is first presented to the reader as an anonymous character; he is an archetypal intrusive stranger from distant places who arrives with a magic potion in his bag which saves, if not the life, at least the reputation of the reigning 'king'. The local people are soon under his spell and he is invested with a strange, legendary romance, 'a man a-come from so far, from the land o' perpetual snow, as we may say, where wolves and wild boars and other dangerous animalcules be as common as blackbirds' (Chapter 8). In truth it is a spurious romance; Farfrae is a level-headed, ambitious young man who leaves his native country to make his fortune. His generous help to Henchard is given freely and with the kindly intention of helping a fellow human being out of a difficulty, but with the full knowledge that he himself will have no further use for his corn-curing process.

Though his career shadows that of Henchard, Farfrae's character is in many ways a contrast to that of the older man; he is cool and canny whilst Henchard is rash; he is even-tempered, moderate and sensible whilst Henchard is hot-tempered, immoderate and often foolish; he is open to innovation whilst Henchard is narrow and old-fashioned; he is gay, attractive and outgoing whilst Henchard is stern, forbidding and withdrawn. Farfrae appears at first to be an exemplary character, the model for every industrious and ambitious young man in Victorian days and it is in this very perfection that our doubts about him lie. Not for him are an imprudent marriage and a wife and child to support before he has the means to support them. More cautious than Michael Henchard in his youth, he sacrifices love for ambition when he rejects the impulse to ask Elizabeth-Jane to marry him, 'I wish I was richer, Miss Newson; and your stepfather had not been offended; I would ask you something in a short time – yes, I would ask you tonight. But that's not for me!' (Chapter 17). What is worse, when he is richer, he sacrifices Elizabeth-Jane for Lucetta. He fails to recognise the true worth of Elizabeth and he fails to recognise the coquetry of Lucetta. When Henchard makes a wrong choice he suffers for it and we identify with him in his suffering; when Farfrae makes a wrong choice someone else suffers for it and he loses our sympathy. The reader responds to him in much the same way as the people of Casterbridge do. When he arrives in the town his gaiety and carefree spirit win him general admiration, but it is not in human nature to love the intruder who begins by gaining a place in our hearts and goes on to gain a position of dominance in our lives. As wealthy corn-factor, as husband of a woman with a doubtful past, as Mayor of the town, he loses in popularity what he has gained in power and riches. Christopher Coney sums it up succinctly as he reflects that, 'Farfrae was still liked in the community; but it must be owned that, as the Mayor and man of money, engrossed with affairs and ambitions, he had lost in the eyes of the poorer inhabitants something of that wondrous charm which he had had for them as a light-hearted penniless young man, who sang ditties as readily as the birds in the trees' (Chapter 37).

It is only when Farfrae himself suffers punishment, learns the pain of loss and endures vicarious shame through the exposure and death of Lucetta that he is saved. He expiates his faults by wooing and marrying

Elizabeth-Jane, but the book ends as it began with Henchard, not with Farfrae. The younger man is, throughout, a foil for his patron. He shows up Henchard's faults; he shadows him in business and in love, replacing him as corn-factor and Mayor and winning and marrying in turn both women whom Henchard had loved in the days of his prosperity. At the same time, his success reflects Henchard's failure and the see-saw of affection which pushes him up and Henchard down when they are man and master reverses its direction when man and master change places.

Richard Newson

Richard Newson, the sailor, though he is an essential element in the plot, is not very fully realised for us. A genial man, he bids for Susan on impulse at the fair; a careful man, he has money in his pocket; a kindly man, he believes Susan will be happier with him than with Michael and so he takes her away. He becomes a generous, loving 'husband', a kindly father, and when he finds that Susan has been disillusioned about the legality of the 'marriage', he effaces himself, disappears, and leaves her to put matters right with her conscience. His dramatic reappearance to Henchard when Lucetta is just dead and Elizabeth-Jane is asleep in the back room shows him to be little changed from the man who paid five guineas on trust for an unknown woman at Weydon-Priors Fair. He accepts Henchard's lie without question and disappears again. On his first appearance he took away Henchard's peace of mind; his final re-appearance to take his rightful place in the wedding ceremony as father of the bride destroys Henchard. Thus, it is as agent of the plot and as part of the novel's pattern that we should look at Newson, not as an individualised character.

Susan Henchard

Of the three women, Susan, though she is perhaps the least regarded is, in many ways, the most remarkable. Courted and married twice by the same man with a nineteen-year interval between, during which she is the common-law wife of another man, she appears to be completely naïve, yet she guards the secret of Elizabeth-Jane's paternity with a persistent cunning, and whilst ensuring that Newson's rights in his daughter are not infringed, she attempts to secure a comfortable future for Elizabeth by concealing from Henchard the death of his own child. Not only this, but she has another plan to fall back on in order to advance the daughter she cherishes, for with a truly conspiratorial skill she writes anonymous letters arranging a chance meeting between Elizabeth and Farfrae in the hope of pushing them towards marriage. Despite this, both the men she lived with believed her to be simple, 'a warm-hearted, home-spun woman . . . not what they call shrewd or sharp at all . . . she could write her own name and no more' (Chapter 41). Was Henchard completely deceived? Did Susan learn to write while she lived with Newson? or has Hardy overlooked the fact that we have evidence of three letters written by her in secret without assistance? It is difficult, if not impossible, to answer these questions for sure.

The opening pages of the book portray Susan as a somewhat mouselike creature, but she is not completely cowed; the spirited rejection of Henchard as she throws her wedding-ring across the furmity tent suggests more to her character than is immediately evident. Her determined effort to find Henchard again and her deception of both her daughter and her husband give further weight to this suggestion. But Susan's character is not fully developed, for like Newson her function is more to further the plot than to be a fully realised individual.

Elizabeth-Jane

Elizabeth-Jane, on the other hand, has a central place in the novel, not only because she is necessary to the plot, but also because she bears a special relationship to author and reader, for Hardy uses her increasingly through the novel as an observer to present scenes, people and ideas to the reader and as a mouthpiece for his own philosophical thoughts on life. He treats her tenderly, clearly liking her; through her eyes we first see Casterbridge, 'an old-fashioned place . . . huddled all together . . . shut in by a square wall of trees, like a plot of garden ground' (Chapter 4), or Joshua Jopp twitching his mouth with anger, bitter disappointment written all over his face when he learns that Henchard has appointed Farfrae as manager in his stead; through her compassion Henchard regains our sympathy when the tide of fortune turns against him and the skimmity-ride, the death of Lucetta and his enmity with Farfrae drive him to the verge of despair; through her we are forced to consider how life allots portions of gaiety, tranquillity and pain, in what proportion and to what extent they are deserved by those who receive them.

Elizabeth is one of those good, simple, innocent women whom Hardy sees buffeted by life and cheated by Time's ironies. In general, moderation is the key to her character. In all her dealings with others she is firm, sensible, but without passion. Her 'goodness' is based on acceptance of Victorian morality which, adhering to herself, she expects others to adhere to. Those who err against this morality she will 'not quite like or respect' (Chapter 24). When Lucetta wins Farfrae's affection away from her she can only reflect on the lesson of renunciation she has learned; when she hears of Lucetta's previous liaison with Henchard, however, she becomes as fierce as an avenging angel, 'Any suspicion of impropriety was to Elizabeth-Jane like a red rag to a bull ... "You ought to marry Mr Henchard or nobody – certainly not another man!"' (Chapter 31). The anger she is unable to arouse on her own behalf is swiftly aroused when propriety and morality are at stake. Her judgement seems hard, but strictly in accordance with justice, if not with mercy or pity. It prepares the reader, however, for Elizabeth's spiritual failure at the end of the book. Our sense of moral goodness is disturbed when Henchard returns on her wedding-day to ask her forgiveness and she rejects him; she is being asked for human pity and she dispenses divine judgement. It is an action based on her understanding of the letter of the law of morality – he has sinned by lying, by cheating her true father and herself, by selfishly trying to snatch his own happiness at the expense of others; but his desperate spiritual need for love and for human communion, his attempt at expiation through self-abasement she cannot recognise; being herself without the grosser forms of sin she cannot comprehend the immensity of the burden they place upon the sinner. So she rejects Henchard and he responds by accepting her judgement and dying. Elizabeth has learned the lesson of mercy too late and she is left at the end of the book with the memory of her own unkindness to sober her happiness.

Lucetta

Lucetta is a type-character who appears in various guises in a number of Hardy's novels. When she comes to Casterbridge she changes her name and attempts to cut herself off from her past. Little of that past is described in the novel; her parents are dead and she lives a rather lonely life until her aunt dies and leaves Lucetta with a comfortable inheritance to set herself up in style as a woman of means. As far as the plot is concerned the most significant thing in her past is her relationship with Henchard, a relationship for which by his account she was largely responsible and which caused a scandal in her native Jersey.

For all her fine airs, Lucetta is flighty and rather foolish. She is, what she denies to Farfrae, a coquette. Having pursued Henchard to Casterbridge, she acts capriciously, at first refusing to see him; by the time she allows him to visit her she has already transferred her affections to Donald Farfrae. Her first meeting with Farfrae in Chapter 23 displays all her arts of coquetry. She persuades him to stay and talk to her by lying to him, she carries on the conversation with a mixture of lies and flattery, she appeals to his sentimental side by speaking on behalf of the lovers about to be parted and ends up with a personal appeal to him not to think ill of her; when he has gone she again refuses to entertain Henchard as visitor, although he had been invited by her. We must, of course, do Lucetta the justice of remembering that she is unaware of the affectionate interest between Elizabeth-Jane and Farfrae, though her determined pursuit first of Henchard and then of Farfrae, and the way in which she makes use of Elizabeth for her own ends suggest this would have made little difference. She is full of arts and wiles: when she is expecting Henchard to call she dresses 'with scrupulous care' and arranges herself 'picturesquely', first in a chair and then on the couch; she puts on her cherry-coloured gown and goes out to confront Farfrae in the market-place where she alone rivals in colour the magnificent new horse-drill which he has brought into Casterbridge for the farmers to view; when she finally promises to marry Henchard she deceives him and goes to Port-Bredy where she marries Farfrae.

Yet Lucetta is not a woman upon whom intrigue sits easily. Her habit of writing letters (a habit stemming from her loneliness and her deserted state in Jersey) makes her vulnerable and finally proves to be her downfall; her thoughtless involvement with Henchard leaves her as much to be pitied as blamed and she proves quite unable to hide her past except by incriminating herself by more letters and by clandestine meetings. Hardy does not depict her very fully; she does not enter the book until almost half way through and the reader is saved from too much sympathy with her by her death.

The rustic chorus

There are no other characters of major significance in the novel, but the group of characters first seen looking in at Henchard presiding over the public dinner in the King's Arms, and later among the company at the Three Mariners listening to Farfrae's songs, deserves some comment. From his earliest novels onwards Hardy had included a number of characters, not easily differentiated one from the other, but making together a 'rustic' or 'comic chorus' which commented on the main action with humour and with a down-to-earth philosophy of life. In *The Mayor of Casterbridge* this chorus comprises Solomon Longways, Christopher Coney, Buzzford and Mother Cuxsom. Though not vital to the plot, they nevertheless serve a significant purpose in helping to place the major characters in a community and by adding a droll humour to the novel. They are ignorant and rough in their manners but they help to emphasise points which Hardy wishes to bring out; for instance, their discussion of Scotland in Chapter 8 underlines the extent to which Farfrae is a stranger among the Wessex people he is soon to work with, or the comments they make on Susan's death (Chapter 18) become general thoughts on the significance of death itself. For the most part, they add little to the plot, though their benevolent interference on Farfrae's behalf before the skimmity-ride is responsible for the confusion which prevents him from arriving home until it is almost too late.

Part 4

Hints for study

Nothing can be a substitute for a thorough and careful reading of *The Mayor of Casterbridge* itself. Once it has been read, the story taken in and a general impression has been received, read it again, giving special attention to particular aspects of the novel. On your second reading take notes and jot down quotations; make sure that your note or quotation is followed by a bracketed page number (or chapter number if you are not using your own book and may have to use a different edition on a subsequent reading). What kind of things will you be looking at as you study the novel more closely? Perhaps you should consider at least some of the following:

(1) characters (especially Michael Henchard)
(2) theme
(3) settings
(4) Hardy's use of nature and the seasonal cycle
(5) superstition
(6) religion
(7) the use of irony
(8) language

Try to think of other interesting or significant aspects of the novel which you could add to this list.

Always remember to return to the text in order to support or illustrate points you are making. Critics may suggest ideas to you, but you should ensure that you accept these ideas only if your own knowledge of the novel confirms them. A critic can be wrong; or two critics may disagree; In Part 3 some points have been discussed where the author of these notes disagrees with other critics and direct reference has been made to what Hardy actually wrote in order to support the argument. Try to make up your own mind by returning to the text yourself and weighing up the evidence.

When we are discussing a novel it is often useful to prompt ourselves by a question, rather than by a statement. For instance if we think about Hardy's settings in this novel we could start ourselves off by saying, 'Hardy adds an historical perspective to his nineteenth-century Wessex settings by constantly referring to the Roman remains in the area', a bald statement which we may be tempted to accept without further investigation, or to prove by looking for evidence (and there is plenty of it) that this is so. Suppose instead we ask ourselves, 'Is it true that Hardy adds an historical perspective to his nineteenth-century Wessex settings by his constant references to the Roman remains in the area?' Now we are forced to answer the question by checking the text, not merely for proof of our statement but to see if it is true. What do we find if we return to the text and look at some of the settings? The first thing we find, in fact, is that it is not only references to old Rome which give such a perspective. Early in Chapter 1 the generalised country setting of Michael's and Susan's journey is universalised in time as well as place by Hardy's comment about the song of a bird (see the first quotation in (2) below). So if we are to collect quotations to illustrate how Hardy deals with historical perspective we realise that we must collect them under at least two headings: (1) references to the old Roman remains; (2) other references. Let us begin to do so:

(1) References to the old Roman remains

(a) 'Casterbridge announced old Rome in every street, alley and precinct. It looked Roman, bespoke the art of Rome, concealed dead men of Rome.' (Chapter 11)

(b) 'The cottage which Mr Henchard hired for his wife Susan . . . was . . . near the Roman wall.' (Chapter 13)

(c) 'Here wheat-ricks overhung the old Roman street.' (Chapter 14)

(d) 'Mrs Henchard's dust mingled with the dust of women who lay ornamented with glass hair-pins and amber necklaces, and men who held in their mouths coins of Hadrian, Posthumus and the Constantines.' (Chapter 20)

(2) Other references

(a) The song of the bird 'might doubtless have been heard on the hill at the same hour, and with the self-same trills, quavers and breves, at any sunset of that season for centuries untold.' (Chapter 1)

(b) 'The spot stretched downward into valleys, and onward to other uplands dotted with barrows, and trenched with the remains of prehistoric forts.' (Chapter 2)

(c) The Three Mariners is described with its 'Elizabethan gables . . . Tudor arch.' (Chapter 6)

(d) Historical continuity is suggested by Hardy relating how 'in 1705 a woman who had murdered her husband was half-strangled and then burnt [in the Roman Amphitheatre] in the presence of ten thousand spectators.' (Chapter 11)

(e) Casterbridge churchyard is 'a churchyard old as civilization.' (Chapter 21)

Whilst we are collecting such references it soon becomes apparent that those which are not about Rome far outnumber those which are. Try to collect more quotations in each category; you will find one or more in Chapters 9, 19, 27, 29, 31, 34, 37, 43, 45 and perhaps elsewhere. Quotations should be kept fairly short and it is useful to learn a few by heart to illustrate aspects of the novel you are interested in.

Could you write an essay on Hardy's settings in *The Mayor of Casterbridge*? We have already collected a good deal of material in the preceding pages. However, you would have to begin by discussing the nineteenth-century Wessex in which the story is placed, illustrating how Hardy juxtaposes descriptions of Casterbridge with comments on the agricultural countryside around in order to show that the town is the complement of the countryside, not a contrast to it. Collect some quotations which describe Casterbridge as a Victorian visitor to the town would have seen it. You will soon find that once more you are able to place your quotations in different categories, for example:

(1) the town itself
(2) the market-place
(3) the Casterbridge Ring.

What other settings are of significance in the novel? In Part 3 attention has been drawn (p.45) to the settings on lonely roads when time and place are hardly emphasised at all; because they are not particularised these scenes help towards a universal interpretation of the story. Look at them again. By now you should have enough material to answer a question on (say) 'Discuss the importance of Hardy's settings in this novel'. Plan out an answer to such a question in note form. Have you considered why Hardy describes Casterbridge so minutely? Or why he establishes the Ring as an eerie, unfriendly place? Or why we generally see the market-place as a picture through a window?

The discussion of Hardy's settings involves discussion of the book as a whole. So does any discussion of the characters, or of Hardy's use of irony or his language. Search out quotations which would help you to answer the following questions:

(1) Discuss the character of Michael Henchard and his relationship with the other principal characters. (Farfrae, Newson, Susan, Elizabeth-Jane, Lucetta.)

(2) What do we know of Michael Henchard as wealthy corn-factor, as Mayor and as public figure? (This involves his relationship with the people of the town and with his workmen.)

(3) Compare the characters of Elizabeth-Jane and Lucetta. (Some consideration of their respective relationships with Henchard and with Farfrae is necessary here.)

(4) 'Fate ensures that Time's ironies punish only Michael Henchard.' Discuss. (Is this really true? Henchard suffers most, but does any main character escape some repercussions from the ironic twists in the plot? Be prepared to disagree with the question if the text does not support its assertions.)

(5) Choose any one example of the dramatic irony in the book and demonstrate its function in the plot as a whole. (In this kind of question beware of simply retelling the story.)

(6) Discuss any aspect of Hardy's use of language in this novel which interests you. (In Part 3 there is a brief discussion of his descriptions, his use of allusions and the problem of dialect and archaic vocabulary; additionally, you could examine his use of dialogue, or the contrasts which are a feature of the book – see, for instance, the last paragraph of Chapter 1 and the first of Chapter 2.)

A good way of getting to know a novel well is by examining a particular major incident and seeing how it bears on theme, plot, character and other aspects of the book. In examining one incident you are forced to examine a number of other incidents as well. We could take as our example here the wife-sale in Chapter 1. The very fact of the sale itself helps to place the novel in a time context, yet the shame Henchard later experiences because of it shows us that it was not generally accepted in society at that time. The sale throws light on the characters of the three main participants – Michael Henchard, the seller, whose ambitions have been thwarted by an early marriage, who at the time of the sale is drunk, and who loses control of his will-power when drunk and is thus surly, ill-tempered and impetuous; Richard Newson, the buyer, a naïve sailor, equally impetuous, but abstemious and good-hearted; Susan, the sold, a simple woman who had borne a great deal, but whose spirit can be roused if she is tried too much. The sale is the starting point for the whole plot. Henchard carried the memory of it around with him in his later life like a secret wound. At what other points in the novel does it impinge directly upon the action? (Look at Chapters 2, 3, 10, 11, 12, 13, 19, 28, 41, 43.) Are you able to categorise its effects under headings so that you can put your material into some sort of order? For instance:

(1) influence on life and character of (a) Michael Henchard; (b) Susan

(2) dramatic turns in the plot; (a) return of Susan, (b) trial of furmity-woman and effect of her disclosure on Henchard and Lucetta, (c) disclosure of Elizabeth-Jane's identity, (d) return of Newson.

You have probably collected enough material by now to write an essay on 'Do you consider the wife-sale in Chapter 1 to be the most important single incident in the book?' Ways in which it affects the plot have been suggested above but you need to use your own judgement as to whether any other incident is of more importance. Perhaps the answers to some of the following questions will help you come to a decision: Would Michael Henchard have become wealthy if Susan and Elizabeth-Jane had stayed with him? Would he have become involved with Lucetta? Would he have met Farfrae in circumstances which would have kept Farfrae in England? Would he have become Mayor of Casterbridge? You hardly need go beyond the answers to these questions; however, consider the effect the *disclosure* of the sale by the furmity-woman had; try to work out how her story altered the course of Henchard's life.

This final section has been designed, not to save you from working, but to help you work more efficiently. For this reason you have been constantly urged in these notes to find things out for yourself, to become well acquainted with Hardy's text and to return to it again and again. Ways of dealing with various questions have been suggested and they have required you to return to the novel's text to collect your material. Here are more questions to consider and model answers to four of them:

(1) Consider the significance of the part played in the novel by either (a) Abel Whittle or (b) the furmity-woman.

(2) Discuss Henchard's use of superstition in this novel.

(3) Choose any three narrative devices to be found in this novel and discuss Hardy's use of them.

(4) Discuss any one incident in the novel which seems to you to throw light on the characters both of (a) Henchard and (b) any one other person.

(5) Consider the part played by letters in this novel.

(6) Discuss the events which lead up to the skimmity-ride and Lucetta's death. What mistakes were made by Henchard, Lucetta and Farfrae and could they have been avoided?

(7) How valuable are the first two chapters to the novel as a whole?

(8) What has this novel to tell us of nineteenth-century Wessex life?

(9) Consider the suitability of the title, *The Mayor of Casterbridge*.

(10) Recommend this novel to a friend, giving substantial reasons why you think he/she should read it.

(11) 'Character is Fate'. Does *The Mayor of Casterbridge* show this to be true?

(12) Are Henchard's misfortunes disproportionate to his sins?

The model answers which follow are the result of considerable preparation. Before the essay is started, and after an initial thorough reading, the text must be skimmed through, notes taken and quotations jotted down. Then an essay plan must be made on the lines suggested earlier in this section. Only then is it possible to write a rough draft of the essay. What appears here is a final, more polished piece of work. Once you have read the essays try to work out the original plan for them.

Model answer to question (1)

Consider the significance of the part played in the novel by (a) Abel Whittle.

Abel Whittle is a very minor character in *The Mayor of Casterbridge*. He is one of Henchard's workmen, a simple, foolish, uneducated man who explains his own ignorance with the comment that 'not being a man o' letters [he] can't read writing' (Chapter 45).

Abel appears only three times in the whole novel. The first time is when, after several warnings, he is late for work and Henchard drags him to the cornyard before he has had time to put his trousers on. This incident leads to the first confrontation between Henchard and Farfrae, in which the corn-factor's rash and passionate action is coolly and rationally resisted by his manager; it is important because it marks the beginning of the rift between the two men, a rift which appears inevitable when the contrast in their characters is considered. A cursory reading may suggest that Henchard is entirely in the wrong, yet Abel Whittle is a very unreliable workman to whom Henchard has offered much indirect kindness, keeping his 'old mother in coals and snuff all the precious winter' (Chapter 15), as the other workmen explain to Farfrae. Henchard's mistake lies first, in his impetuosity and secondly, in his stubbornness, for his punishment of Abel is too extreme and Farfrae is surely right to assume that he has learned his lesson and to send him home to dress properly. The moment of pathos which ends the incident betrays Henchard's basic insecurity: 'Why did you speak to me before them like that, Farfrae? You might have stopped till we were alone'. It is not Farfrae's reproof, but its public nature, which appears to Henchard to undermine his position as master.

The second appearance of Abel is considerably later in the book when Henchard's business has passed to Farfrae. Abel is seen talking briefly to Elizabeth-Jane, explaining to her the difference between the two men as masters: Henchard's roughness and anger always made him afraid, yet he was paid more; with Farfrae, on the other hand, life is more peaceful, but he makes the men work harder and pays them 'a shilling a week less' (Chapter 31). Again the reader senses a generous disposition behind Henchard's stern exterior and cannot help drawing a contrast between his kindly intentions and Farfrae's hard-headed and more mercenary attitude. Yet Henchard is betrayed again and again by the uncertainty of his temper, and his workmen appear to give him little credit for his generosity, though early in the book Solomon Longways emphasises his fairness, commenting, 'Mr Henchard has never cussed me unfairly ever since I've worked for 'n' (Chapter 5).

Abel's final appearance is in the very last scene of the novel, for it is he who follows and assists Henchard in his misery and desolation. It is Abel who ministers to him, finding him shelter, providing him with a bed and preparing him food, and when he dies it is Abel who is left to arrange his burial until Farfrae and Elizabeth-Jane arrive on the scene. The simple fidelity of poor Abel is very moving and serves to intensify the tragedy; it is his attempt to repay Henchard's rough kindness, as he explains to Henchard himself, 'Ye wer kind-like to mother if ye were rough to me, and I would fain be kind-like to you' (Chapter 45). This remark recalls to the reader the comments of the other workmen when Henchard punished Abel for being late and reminds us of Henchard's kindlier side. The sympathy and compassion of Abel Whittle contrasts with Elizabeth-Jane's spiritual failure at the end and teaches her the one lesson she needs to learn, for he repays both Henchard's kindness and his harshness with mercy, pity and forgiveness, kindly human virtues which Elizabeth in her moral indignation had allowed to be sacrificed to her idea of justice.

Model answer to Question (5)

Consider the part played by letters in this novel.

Letters have served as a useful narrative device since the novel began. Richardson in *Pamela* (1740–1) tells his story almost entirely through letters and in *Pride and Prejudice* (1813) Jane Austen makes considerable use of letters to further her plot. In *The Mayor of Casterbridge* many of the twists in the plot are preceded by the discovery of the contents of a letter.

In general, the letters are of two kinds: first, the short businesslike letter which is written and delivered and makes its impact straight away; secondly, the letter which is written and kept by either the writer or the recipient until a later date.

The first letter in the novel is the short note written by Farfrae to Henchard explaining that the 'grown wheat' could be partially restored. This note has far-reaching consequences, for it results in Farfrae's abandoning his intention to travel to America and staying in Casterbridge to become Henchard's manager.

Other examples of this kind of letter are the notes exchanged between Susan and Henchard when she arrives in Casterbridge; these result first in Susan's being established in a cottage and eventually in a second marriage between the couple. Or again, there are the letters from Henchard to Farfrae about Elizabeth-Jane, first forbidding him to court her and then giving him permission to do so. Farfrae's attempt to see Elizabeth after the second of these letters introduces him to Lucetta, with all the fateful consequences which follow that meeting.

The other kind of letter introduces mystery and suspense into the plot. Chapter 18 of the novel, a short chapter in itself, is significant because of the interest aroused by two such letters. One is from Lucetta to Henchard asking for the return of 'those letters with which I pestered you day after day in the heat of my feelings'. This bundle of passionate letters is not returned to the writer, however, because she fails to keep the appointment she makes. Whilst the reader is left wondering what will happen to these letters, yet another mystery is introduced, for Susan, dying, writes a letter to her husband which she locks up after directing that it shall not be opened until Elizabeth-Jane's wedding-day.

The mystery of Susan Henchard's letter is cleared up in the following chapter, but it is responsible for the cruellest and most ironic stroke of fate against Michael Henchard, for he has no sooner claimed Elizabeth-Jane as his own daughter than the letter discloses to him that she is not his child but Newson's. His hopes of salvaging some human love from the wreck of his personal life turn to dust and ashes; Susan is dead, Lucetta, he believes, gone from him and now Elizabeth is lost to him. The repercussions from this letter echo through the rest of the book.

The bundle of letters from Lucetta is apparently forgotten in the events which follow Susan's death. Henchard, ruined and bankrupt, goes to live with Jopp; Lucetta marries Farfrae and moves into the house which Henchard had previously occupied; the relationship between Farfrae and Henchard deteriorates until on Henchard's side it approaches naked enmity. Yet all this time Lucetta's letters are not mentioned. Then, at last, she feels that she must ask for their return again. Her request brings about a crisis, for Henchard is sorely tempted to disclose their contents to Farfrae. The better side of his nature prevails, however, and he is persuaded to send the letters back to Lucetta. His method of doing so results in Lucetta's death, for Henchard entrusts the bundle to Joshua Jopp who opens the letters and reads them aloud to the company in Peter's Finger. The knowledge they gain from the letters persuades them to prepare a 'skimmity-ride' with Lucetta and Michael Henchard as the effigies and this is directly responsible for Lucetta's death.

Thus it can be seen that letters move the plot along in various ways and serve a useful narrative purpose in this novel.

Model answer to Question (8)

What has this novel to tell us of nineteenth-century Wessex life?

Life in Wessex in the nineteenth century was very different from what it is today. The principal difference lies in the mechanisation which has taken place. The mode of travel in *The Mayor of Casterbridge* is by horse and carriage or on foot; the novel opens with Michael and Susan Henchard trudging towards Weydon-Priors along a dirt road so thick with dust that it deadened 'their footfalls like a carpet'. The poor generally travelled on foot and often long distances were covered in this way. Susan and Elizabeth-Jane also travelled mainly on foot, though they were occasionally helped on their journey, 'sometimes on farmers' wagons, sometimes in carriers' vans'. Donald Farfrae and Lucetta Templeman, on the other hand, on their first appearance in the novel, are able to afford to travel by coach, the horse-drawn bus service of the nineteenth century. Richer and more settled people used their own small horse-drawn carriages and this is how Donald and Elizabeth-Jane travel around the countryside to look for Henchard in the last chapter.

The other aspect of life in which the lack of mechanisation is apparent is in the methods of farming which are followed by the Wessex people. The Casterbridge shops sell the tools and implements which are necessary for the farmers and farm-workers in the neighbouring countryside, but they are things designed for manual work – scythes and hoes, wheelbarrows and hedging-gloves. When an early agricultural machine, the horse-drill, is introduced by Farfrae for exhibition in the market, it causes great interest and wonder, for sowing had always until that time been done by hand.

Hardy shows his reader something of the occupations followed by the men of Wessex in the nineteenth century, from the simple country trades such as those of hay-trusser and turnip-hoer to the more influential business pursuits such as corn-merchant or manager. In general, men's occupations are concerned with producing the necessities of life, growing corn and making bread, not with manufacturing comforts or luxuries.

As men's jobs are fairly simple, so are their leisure pursuits. They drink and smoke in the local inns and entertain themselves with songs; they go to church on Sundays and at times of celebration they create their own festivals; thus both Farfrae and Henchard organise entertainments for the townsfolk with dancing and contests such as climbing greasy poles or wheelbarrow races. Not all their pleasures are so open-hearted, however; some of the townsfolk are quite ready to indulge in more sinister activities, as the carefully planned 'skimmity-ride' indicates.

What we see in Hardy's Casterbridge is the life of a closely-knit community, each group depending on the labours of the others; in the small market town most people know each other; when a problem such as that of Henchard's 'grown wheat' arises it affects everyone; when a celebration such as that of Farfrae's marriage to Lucetta takes place the whole town rejoices. Men are able to make money and lose money fast; the man who rises by his own efforts is respected, but little pity is shown to him when he falls. The view of life is an unsentimental one in which joy and misery come to rich and poor alike and the novel's tragic outcome prevents us from idealising the rural life of that time.

Model answer to Question (11)

'Character is Fate'. Does *The Mayor of Casterbridge* show this to be true?

When Hardy quotes Novalis's comment that 'Character is Fate' he is describing how everything that Farfrae puts his hand to seems to prosper. However, the quotation has a wider implication in the novel as a whole; the book is sub-titled 'A Story of a Man of Character' and it is Henchard, the Man of Character himself, who dominates the plot.

On a number of occasions Fate appears to intervene, but it is never the prime mover; the action of the story is governed by the characters; the order of events relies on what they are and do, not on chance or Fate. At the very outset when Newson enters the furmity tent at the precise moment that the farce of the auction appears to be coming to an end without catastrophe, it is Henchard's drunken obstinacy, combined with Susan's simplicity, that allows the auction to take place. Likewise, it is Henchard's shame and embarrassment which prevent him from making proper enquiries about Susan and the sailor the next day. A wife more assertive would have halted the auction before the transaction with Newson took place; a husband less impetuous would never have started it.

The time when Fate does indeed seem to be against Henchard is the evening when he decides to tell Elizabeth that he is her father. Susan is dead and he now wants to claim his daughter as his own; as delicately as possible he retells the story of his first marriage to the woman he married a second time nineteen years later; he tells the girl that she is his daughter long lost to him and promises to produce proof of his story. In his search for proof he finds Susan's letter which proves to him not his own paternity, but that Elizabeth is Newson's daughter. The irony of this fateful timing makes Henchard believe 'that the concatenation of events this evening had produced was the scheme of some sinister intelligence bent on punishing him'. Yet Hardy himself asserts that the events had developed naturally since it was Henchard's search for proof of his story that led to his discovery and there is no doubt that the protagonists themselves are responsible for the whole sequence of events. Had Susan had the courage to tell her husband the truth or, having deceived him, had she allowed her secret to be buried with her, Henchard would have continued to believe that Elizabeth was his daughter. Had he not treated Susan's dying wish so lightly he would not have read the letter until the girl was married.

The novel is full of incidents which show that man is master of his own fate. It is chance which brings Farfrae to Casterbridge, but it is Henchard who persuades him to stay; ill luck decrees that the old furmity-woman's disclosures occur the day after Lucetta has unwillingly agreed to marry Henchard, but it is his harshness and violence that cause her to hasten her marriage to Farfrae.

Thus, throughout the novel, Hardy shows again and again that, though luck may appear to be on the side of one man and against another, events are governed by character and not by Fate.

Part 5

Suggestions for
further reading

The text

The best text is that of the New Wessex Edition (Macmillan, London, 1974). Annotated by Bryn Caless, this has a useful introductory essay by Ian Gregor.

Thomas Hardy's life

GITTINGS, ROBERT: *Young Thomas Hardy,* Heinemann, London, 1975. A study of Hardy's life up to just after the time of his first marriage.
— *The Later Hardy,* Heinemann, London, 1977. This volume covers the period of Hardy's second marriage up to his death.
HARDY, FLORENCE EMILY: *The Life of Thomas Hardy, 1840–1928,* Macmillan, London, 1962. Although published under his wife's name, originally in two volumes (1928 and 1930), this work is now generally acknowledged to have been written by Hardy himself; though not always strictly accurate, it is an invaluable documentation of Hardy's life.
WILLIAMS, MERRYN: *A Preface to Hardy,* Longman, London, 1976. The first half of this book is a well-written brief life of Hardy, carefully placing him both historically and in his own Wessex setting.

Critical studies

BROWN, DOUGLAS: *Hardy: The Major of Casterbridge,* Studies in English Literature, Edward Arnold, London, 1962. A good, straightforward short study of the novel, examining the story and its setting and looking briefly at characterisation.
GREGOR, IAN: *The Great Web, The Form of Hardy's Major Fiction,* Faber, London, 1974. A detailed study of Hardy's six major novels.
GUERARD, A. J.: *Thomas Hardy: The Novels and Stories,* Harvard University Press, Cambridge, Mass., 1949. A general account of Hardy's work with a modern critical approach.
MILLGATE, MICHAEL: *Thomas Hardy, His Career as a Novelist,* Bodley Head, London, 1971. Another general book on Hardy which looks at his work in a balanced and scholarly way.

PINION, F. B.: *A Hardy Companion*, Macmillan, London, 1968. An excellent reference book which helps to elucidate many aspects of the novels. The 1976 reprint has some alterations and contains an updated bibliographical section.

VIGAR, PENELOPE: *The Novels of Thomas Hardy*, Athlone Press, London, 1974. A very readable critical survey.

Other books referred to in the text

BROOKS, JEAN: *Thomas Hardy: The Poetic Structure*, Elek, London, 1971.

PAGE, NORMAN: *Thomas Hardy*, Routledge and Kegan Paul, London, 1977.

The author of these notes

HILDA D. SPEAR was educated at Furzedown College of Education, London, the University of London, and the University of Leicester. She has taught in various schools, colleges of education and universities, including Purdue University, Indiana. She is now a Senior Lecturer in the Department of English, the University of Dundee. Her publications include *Remembering, We Forget* (1979); an annotated edition of *The English Poems of C. S. Calverley* (1974); and *The Poems and Selected Letters of Charles Hamilton Sorley* (1978). She wrote the biographical and bibliographical section of *The Pelican Guide to English Literature V*, and she has published articles on teaching English as well as on R. H. Barham, C. S. Calverley, W. M. Praed, Ford Madox Ford, Wilfred Owen, Isaac Rosenberg and Siegfried Sassoon.